PLANET OF PERIL

Derring-do on a world of primitive monsters!

When Robert Grandon swapped bodies with a prince of the planet Venus, he was concerned only with the thrill and interest of living on a different world. But the situation he found himself in was hardly that of a leisurely sightseer. Instead, he found himself smack in the center of a whirlwind of intrigue, danger, and desperation.

Planet of Peril is a science-fiction adventure on a world of semi-barbaric nations, ferocious beasts, gigantic reptiles, and maidens in distress!

PLANET OF PERIL

OTIS ADELBERT KLINE

WILDSIDE PRESS

PLANET OF PERIL

Published in 2007 by Wildside Press.
www.wildsidepress.com

CHAPTER I

Robert Ellsmore Grandon stifled a yawn with difficulty as the curtain went down on the first act of *Don Giovanni* and wondered what was the matter. It wasn't that opera bored him, or that tonight's performance was inferior; in fact, what he had been able to give his attention to struck him as being among the best performances he had seen. But something was distracting him, something he could not put his finger on; and the effort to keep his attention on the music and the performers was tiring him. Perhaps it was just one of those days, he thought.

He was tired of life at twenty-four, he decided — tired and disillusioned and somehow trapped. After his spell of military service, he'd broken away from family obligations and expectations to join revolutionaries in Cuba. The struggle there had seemed important, worth risking his neck for; but he'd seen, much earlier than some others, that the new regime was just a change of masters. He'd gotten out while getting out was easy and returned to take up the career in insurance administration that his uncle wanted him to take — the uncle who had paid his college expenses. Now, Robert and Vincent Grandon would prepare for the position that Uncle Arthur would be leaving in a few years. It would be a good career for both young men; for while only one could step into Arthur Grandon's shoes, the second spot would be no less desirable.

Very likely, with full effort, he could make the top — but his cousin had the extra measure of devotion to the business that Robert Grandon simply couldn't bring. Robert Ellsmore Grandon yearned for action, adventure, romance — something that seemed to be gone in the world of the Twentieth Century.

He made his way to the bar thinking that he'd chuck it all in a moment for a chance to think and act for himself, for a chance to accomplish something worthwhile according to his own lights. Yes — insurance was worthwhile, he thought as he sat at the bar and beckoned to Louis, but not worth *his* while.

Louis looked his way, nodded, and started to mix a gibson for him. The bartender had a curious grin on his face as he set the glass down. "Did you get the message, Mr. Grandon?"

Robert Grandon blinked. "What message?"

"Didn't you see the papers today?"

Grandon shook his head. "Just glanced at them. What's up?"

Louis went back and bent down, to return with the *Times*, folded to a certain page, and placed it on the bar before him. To

Grandon's astonishment, he saw a sketch of himself staring him in the face.

"Had you planned in advance to come tonight, Mr. Grandon?"

Grandon looked up with a puzzled expression on his face. "No — now that you mentioned it, I hadn't. I was going to ask a friend to come with me next Friday night. Came down this morning to see about tickets, and decided that I'd come tonight alone, when I found that there was a good seat available . . . Don't know why, now that I think of it."

Louis' face wore a strange smile. "Read that ad, Mr. Grandon. Maybe you are the one."

Grandon picked up the paper. The heading read, *"I Want You!"* There was no caption under the sketch; beneath it, the text said: "I do not know your name, or anything about you, except that you are in the city. I want to perform an experiment, and you may be the man I need. If you are, you will know by these tokens.

"You will feel an urge to go to a certain place tonight which you may or may not have been planning to go to, and you will want to get there around 8 P.M. Starting at 8:30 P.M., every half hour, I will send you a message. You may not hear it the first or second time, but you may feel distracted. If you are the man I want, it will seem as if a voice is speaking to you. It will be a voice in your mind; it will say 'Doctor Morgan' and direct you to go to a particular spot. There a man will be waiting for you; he will ask you a question which I shall also tell you of when I communicate with you. Please give him a hearing before you decide."

"Looks as if you've gotten the first part of it, Mr. Grandon. You hadn't expected to come tonight, but here you are."

Grandon put the newspaper down. It *had* been just about half an hour after the performance started that he'd begun to feel distracted and a little irritated.

Louis said, "It's two minutes to nine, Mr. Grandon. Maybe you'll get the message this time."

Grandon sipped the gibson, with his eyes on the clock. He tried to relax, to let himself open to whatever thoughts might come into his head. He'd heard of experiments in telepathy, and while he didn't find parapsychology too convincing, he had no strong bias against it. In fact, he'd thought that it might be fascinating if this sort of thing could be so. Here would be a new frontier if . . .

It wasn't exactly a whisper, but there was a softness about a voice he now seemed to hear yet not to hear. It said, "Doctor Morgan." Grandon sat up straight. Again it came: "Doctor Morgan." A third time; then the voice said, "Go to the telephone booths in the lobby. A man wearing a tuxedo with a green lapel pin will offer you a cigarette."

The voice ceased. Grandon waited a moment or two, but there was nothing more.

"Did you get it, Mr. Grandon?" asked Louis eagerly.

Grandon finished his gibson and put a bill down on the bar. "Could be," he said. "I have a pretty good imagination, you know. Think I'll wait another half hour and see."

He left the bar. Either this was or it wasn't. If it was, then he might as well follow up now as wait another half-hour. If it wasn't, it didn't make any difference; he couldn't possibly pay any attention to the opera now, no matter who was singing.

He made his way to the phone booths in the lobby and looked around, oblivious to the feminine eyes that turned to glance at his broad shoulders and curly black hair. No one fitting the description he'd received was in sight. He waited a moment and began to feel foolish.

Just imagination, he decided a little sadly. Well, there was time for a cigarette before he had to get back to his seat. He was reaching for his case when a pleasant voice at his right said, "Try one of mine, won't you?"

Grandon turned and looked into the smiling eyes of a man about his own age. A man wearing a tuxedo with a green lapel pin. He accepted with thanks.

"Excellent performance, don't you think?" volunteered the smiling one, lighting a cigarette himself which he had, unnoticed by Grandon in his confusion, taken from the side of the case opposite the one which he had extended a moment before.

"I suppose so — ah — why, yes, of course . . ."

Grandon was beginning to feel unaccountably drowsy.

Suddenly he slumped forward, and would have fallen on his face, but for the quick assistance of the friendly young man. A moment later he lost consciousness.

An attendant came running up. "What's the matter with your friend?" he asked.

"Fainted dead away. It's his heart; he's had spells like this quite often lately. Help me get him outdoors."

The two of them carried Grandon outside, followed by the more curious bystanders. When he reached the sidewalk, the young man waved to the driver of a car parked on the other side of the street. It immediately swung across and drew up to the curb.

"Let's put him in the car," said the young man. "I'm used to this — a spin on Michigan Boulevard will revive him. Just needs fresh air. His doctor has told me how to handle him."

They lifted Grandon into the car and the driver put the top down. The young man handed a crisp bill to the attendant and got into the car, which drove away.

CHAPTER II

When Grandon regained consciousness he was lying on a cot in a dimly lighted room. He looked about him in bewilderment as he saw four bare concrete walls, a heavy oak door studded with many large bolts, and a small window fitted with powerful iron bars more than an inch in diameter.

There was a chair and a small table with a lamp on it next to the cot. On the table, Grandon saw a sheet of paper. He rolled over and picked it up, switching on the lamp.

"Dear Mr. Grandon," he read, *"I must admit and apologize for technically kidnapping you; but I hope to be able to persuade you shortly that this was both necessary and to your advantage. Now I must ask you to be patient for a little while; I shall see you soon. The drug you were given should be wearing off by evening — you were kidnapped last night — and I can assure you that it will have no harmful after-effects, physical or mental."* The paper was signed, *"Dr. Morgan."*

Grandon arose and tottered unsteadily toward the door. It was evidently locked from the outside, for he could not rattle it. He went to the window and peered out. Night had fallen, and a myriad of twinkling stars looked down at him from a clear sky. Not a tree, house, or earthly object of any kind was visible. There was only the starry sky above and the black void below.

He heard the sound of talking, and wheeled about as a bolt slid back and the door opened. Two men entered. The foremost was tall and of large structure; his forehead was high and bulged outward, so that his shaggy eyebrows, which grew together above the bridge of his aquiline nose, half-concealed his eyes. He wore a pointed, closely-cropped beard, in which a few gray hairs proclaimed him as middle-aged. Behind him was the young man who had given him the drugged cigarette in the lobby of the opera house.

The young man advanced and extended his hand. "How are you feeling now, Mr. Grandon?" he asked. "Ah, you seem surprised that we know your name. That will be explained to you. I should have introduced myself sooner. My name is Harry Thorne. Allow me to present Doctor Morgan."

The big man held out his hand and said in a booming bass voice, "This is a pleasure I have long anticipated, Mr. Grandon."

It was nothing like the voice he had heard in his mind, and yet it was the same voice. Grandon realized that at once; and his curiosity, added to the feeling of confidence in these men's intentions toward him that the note had imparted, washed away any resentment he might feel at their methods. He clasped the doctor's muscular hand and muttered an acknowledgement.

"And now," said Morgan, "if you will accompany us to dinner, we shall start the explanation due you. Afterwards, I shall ask you to read two interesting manuscripts before we talk further; they will tell you far more, and prepare you far better, for the experiment I have in mind than a lecture from me."

In Dr. Morgan's drawing room, where night had given way to day while Robert Ellsmore Grandon read two novel-length manuscripts, Dr. Morgan — who had entered just as Grandon was finishing the last chapter of the second box of neatly-typed pages — smiled at his guest quizzically. "What do you think of them?" he asked.

Grandon shook his head. "If I hadn't had the experience of the past day or so, I'd think they were just good stories and nothing more. Even so, they sound fantastic."

"They are," Morgan agreed. "But nonetheless true. To summarize briefly, I started experimenting with telepathy ten years ago, and finally succeeded in building a device which would pick up and amplify thought waves."

"And thought waves, you found," said Grandon, "are not limited to space or time. So you picked up the waves projected by another man who had built a similar device to project them — only this man was on Mars."

"But not the present-day Mars — the Mars of some millions of years ago, when a high human civilization did exist there." *

"And you and this Martian scientist, Lal Vak, found that persons who are nearly doubles in physical appearance may have similar brain-patterns — enough alike so that consciousness may be exchanged between them. Your first experiment involved such an exchange between an Earthman named Harry Thorne and a Martian named Borgen Takkor. The man you call Harry Thorne was born on Mars as Borgen Takkor, while the true Harry Thorne is 'now' living on Mars — and leading a most adventurous and satisfying career from the account I have read."

Dr. Morgan nodded. "He and his princess have had many adventures together beyond those related in the first manuscript. To us, of course, both have been dead millions of years. But it is possible for me to tune in on their lives at any point where Harry was transmitting to me. He has never regretted his choice."

* See The Swordsman of Mars by Otis Adelbert Kline.

"Then," went on Grandon, "you got in touch with a Venusian named Vorn Vangal, who is a contemporary of Lal Vak and Borgen Takkor. With his help you constructed a space-time vehicle through which your nephew, Jerry Morgan, was able to go to Mars in the flesh. And he, too, made out pretty well." *

Morgan nodded. "Yes. I sent Jerry to Mars that way, and hoped that I'd be able to send someone to Venus the same way. But my telekinetic control failed in some way on the return trip, and I never recovered the ship I built for Jerry. Vorn Vangal said he would build one on Venus and send it to Earth for me, so that I could visit him, but I do not know when this will be possible. It may be soon; it may not be for some years." Morgan smiled. "And I'm not too patient a man. I know that it is possible for me to get an account of Venus as seen by Earthmen's eyes — the Venus that was, in relation to the Mars that was — just as I learned about Mars in those two manuscripts you've read. So I asked Vorn Vangal if he could send me the brain waves of two Venusians, to see if I could find their counterparts here on Earth. Then Harry urged me to try to see if there was a Venusian with whom he could change personalities — so I sent his picture and brainwave pattern to Vorn Vangal."

"I see. And Vorn Vangal sent you the picture and brainwave pattern of a Venusian who was — me."

"Yes. You'll recall that Lal Vak had shown me how to construct a mind-compass, which would indicate whether there were any living persons here on Earth whose brainwaves corresponded with those of the Martians whose pictures he sent me. This would not only aid in my finding such people here on Earth, it would also protect me from disappointment on coming across someone who looked right, but whose brain-pattern did not match closely enough for an exchange of personalities, after all."

"Has that happened?" Grandon asked.

"Only once. But now it's all arranged for Harry; and I hope you'll be interested in going to Venus, too."

Grandon smiled. "After reading those two accounts of conditions on Mars, I certainly am. Of course, I suppose it's nothing like Venus."

"There are differences, of course, but the civilizations are on a somewhat similar level. The planet is known as Zarovia, and your physical counterpart is a gentleman who has been enslaved by an Amazon ruler — a princess with no thought save of her own pleasure. He finds it impossible to escape from bondage, and is there-

*See *The Outlaws of Mars* by Otis Adelbert Kline, Avalon Books, 1960.

fore willing to make the exchange. Mr. Thorne's bodily duplicate is a prince of a realm on the opposite side of the planet from that occupied by the slave. The prince has been petted and pampered and shielded from all danger, and longs for adventure; he is willing to exchange bodies for a time with Mr. Thorne . . . Well, what do you say? Are you willing to make the trip?"

Grandon smiled. "You know, Doctor, I'm a little surprised. You investigated the Earth-born Harry Thorne very carefully, because you'd made a bad choice and sent a criminal to Mars ahead of him. You knew your nephew thoroughly because you were in telepathic communication with him for years, though he didn't know it then. But what do you think about me?"

"Touché!" chuckled Morgan. "I forgot to tell you. I've gone a good ways beyond telepathic projection in the last few years. When I contacted your mind, I also got a very full picture of your character and personality — no intimate details, but sufficient to assure me that you were the sort of man I wanted. And that you were very likely to go along with me if the way could be cleared for you . . . But suppose you tell me of any inhibiting factors; I think they can be cleared up."

Robert Ellsmore Grandon recounted his personal situation briefly, and Morgan nodded. "Yes," he said. "This checks with the information I've gathered on Mr. Arthur Grandon since you arrived here. He's sincerely devoted to you, you know. I don't believe he'll stand in the way if he knows you want to go on some caper of your own and by your own choice . . . Suppose you phone him long distance now. Here's what I suggest you tell him . . ."

"You were right, Doctor," Grandon said after bidding his uncle farewell. "Uncle Arthur agrees that Vincent is better suited to handle the firm than I. He just wanted me to try for awhile and see — says he half expected something like this when I disappeared and was concerned lest I forget to let him know."

"Then we need waste no more time, Mr. Grandon."

"But — my body will remain here while my personality goes to Venus. What happens to it?"

"You need have no fear about that. The man who comes to inhabit it — forgotten about him, haven't you? — will naturally be careful of it; for if he loses it there will be no return for him, either to this world or his own."

"What do we have to do in order to exchange bodies? And how will you keep in touch with me?"

"I will, at regular intervals, establish telepathic rapport with you and Thorne while you are asleep. You will know nothing of these telepathic communications — which will be as detailed as those you read last night — unless I see fit to convey a message to you which will probably come in the form of a dream, so vivid that you will remember every detail. If you wish to communicate with me for any reason whatever, I will learn of it when I establish rapport with you."

Grandon smiled. "I'm ready. Want me to lie down and look into a mirror the way Harry Thorne did when you sent him to Mars?"

"Right. And the present Harry Thorne will follow you in a few hours — you may meet on Venus, though it isn't too likely." He set up the mirror, painted with alternate circles of red and black, as Grandon reposed on the sofa. "Now think of Venus, far off in time and space — millions of miles, millions of years away . . ."

CHAPTER III

Robert Ellsmore Grandon was awakened from a sound sleep by a shaft of brilliant sunlight which shone through the mica-paneled window of the quarry-slaves' sleeping quarters. He blinked, turned uneasily, then sat up. His muscles appeared stiff and bruised and his back smarted and burned. He noticed that his sole articles of apparel consisted of a scarlet breechcloth and a pair of sandals of strange design. His face was covered with a thick, black beard, and his hair was matted and unkempt.

He rose stiffly and walked to the window, hoping for a clear view of a Zarovian landscape, but he was disappointed, for in front of his window there stretched a solid wall of black marble cliffs. The only visible vegetation consisted of a few pink toadstool-like growths which grew from niches in the rock, some over twelve feet in height.

He turned and glanced at his roommates. Fifty men were quartered in the sleeping shed. The bedding consisted of a coarse, dried moss, which made an exceptionally resilient couch. The men were attired like Grandon, except that their breechcloths were gray instead of scarlet. Their skins were sunburned like his own, and marked with scars and open wounds.

Grandon was startled by a hollow booming sound, and someone on the outside opened a large door at the center of the shed. Instantly every man sprang to his feet, and he saw that they were forming in single file to march through the door. He joined the procession, which was heading for a large building in the midst of a group of sheds similar to the one he had occupied, and saw that the sound emanated from a large cylinder of iron suspended from a steel beam in front of the building, and beaten by a man who wielded a large club wrapped with thongs.

Heavily-armed guards stood at intervals of about fifty feet on either side of their pathway. Each guard carried a tall spear with a broad blade about four feet long; a sword with a basket hilt, its blade rather like that of a scimitar, hung from the left side of the belt.

From the right depended a weapon which was utterly strange to Grandon. It was about two feet long, oblong like a carpenter's level, and apparently composed of blued steel. A rivet passed completely through it about four inches from the end, holding it firmly to the belt, although it could be tilted at any angle, and its wearer could point it in any direction by turning his body.

Grandon had yet to learn the efficiency of this weapon, the

tork, which fired needlelike glass projectiles filled with a potent poison that paralyzed man and beast alike almost as soon as it penetrated, and had a range as great as the most powerful of rifles. These tiny bullets were propelled by a highly explosive gas, ignited by an electric spark at the touch of a button.

The gas was compressed in a chamber at the rear of the tork, while the glass missiles were held in a magazine near the muzzle. After a shot was fired, the weapon would automatically reload, a bullet sliding into place in front while just the right charge of gas was released in the chamber behind it. Each tork held a thousand rounds of ammunition.

The slaves passed through the building where each man had his ration doled out to him: a bowl of stewed mushrooms and a steaming cup of a beverage which Grandon found to be very much like a strong wine.

As he followed his companions, Grandon noticed that each man stopped before a small shrine and stood for a moment with head bowed low and hand extended toward it, palm downward. When he reached the shrine, he stopped as the others had done, then gave a gasp of amazement at the life-sized painting of the most beautiful woman he had ever seen.

She wore a robe of scarlet, ornamented with gold and precious stones, and a jeweled band of platinum imprisoned a mass of golden curls which were piled on top of her head after a style different from anything he had ever seen. She was seated on a massive golden throne with cushions of scarlet, across the arms of which rested a scarbo — a sword like those carried by the guards, but with a hilt of gold studded with rubies.

Could this be the Amazon ruler of whom Dr. Morgan had spoken?

A sharp exclamation brought him to his senses; he turned and saw an overseer advancing with whip upraised. Quickly bowing as the others had done, he ran forward to join his fellow slaves.

Once outside the building, the men seated themselves on the ground in little scattered groups for their morning meal. Grandon joined a company of those who had occupied the same dormitory with him.

He could not take part in the general conversation because the language was unintelligible to him — yet the words sounded strangely familiar. A recollection of their meaning was stored in the brain cells of the body which had become his, but the ego which was Grandon could not interpret them. He kept silent and listened.

The meal finished, the slaves were herded to the quarries by their drivers. Each driver, who had charge of ten slaves, wore both tork and scarbo in his belt and carried a whip, the five lashes of which were woven from some coarse fiber and interwoven with short pieces of a brittle, nettlelike moss, which broke off in the skin of the victim, inflicting pain like that of a thousand bee stings.

Grandon managed to keep pace with his fellow slaves. The intense heat of the sun would have made labor in the open impossible, had it not been constantly tempered by the floating clouds of vapor, ever present in the dense, moist Zarovian atmosphere.

The marble was being removed from the hillside in large rectangular blocks, by thousands of slaves working on a series of terraces, each of which was the height of one of the blocks. The crews were so distributed that the terraced hillside constantly retained the same general contour.

Grandon's crew worked on the bottom terrace all morning, but were ordered to the top in the afternoon to reinforce the laborers in that section who, for some reason, had not kept up their quota. He and a fellow slave were removing one of the heavy blocks by means of levers when his end slipped and fell on another block, breaking off a large fragment. The driver raised his whip and struck Grandon a stinging blow across the shoulders.

Quickly wheeling, Grandon landed a tremendous right hook on the point of the man's jaw. It was a clean knock-out. Another driver came running with whip upraised, but Grandon bowled him over with a marble fragment and ran through the group of startled slaves toward the brow of the hill. Someone raised the alarm and a half dozen torks were immediately pointed toward the fugitive. Several slaves fell, struck by the missiles intended for him, as he disappeared over the hilltop.

Before him stretched a dense, waving forest of tree ferns into which he plunged without slacking his speed, his pursuers close behind. As he dodged in and out among the tree trunks he could hear their halloos growing fainter and fainter; finally, no sound was audible except the rustling of the countless, wind-shaken fern leaves.

He slackened his pace and, after proceeding about a mile farther, stopped and looked about him.

Huge tree ferns with rough trunks and foliage growing out of the top like that of palm trees, some of them over seventy feet in height, towered above the shorter, more bushy varieties which were themselves giants. Then there were climbing ferns hanging in tangled masses, creeping ferns, and dwarf, low-growing kinds, barely raising their fronds above the thick carpet of moss which everywhere covered the forest floor.

Grandon noticed that the ground slanted slightly toward his right, and intuition told him that this might lead to a valley and water. He changed his course accordingly. He hoped also to find some fruit, berries or nuts with which to satisfy his hunger.

As he trudged wearily forward, sunset was succeeded by twilight, and before he realized it, the black, moonless Zarovian night had spread its impenetrable mantle about him.

Suddenly, from out of the darkness behind him, came a peal of horrible, demoniac laughter.

As he wheeled, two glowing phosphorescent orbs were slowly advancing as if something were creeping or slinking toward him. Then, without warning, the hideous noise was repeated at his left.

He turned to face another pair of menacing eyes, then leaped for the trunk of the nearest tree-fern and climbed it barely in time to escape the snapping jaws that yawned beneath him.

Not until he had reached the leaf-crown, fifty feet above the ground, did he pause or look downward. Then he saw, not two, but a dozen pairs of eyes glancing toward him, while peal after peal of the nerve-racking laughter smote his ears.

Time dragged along. What manner of things were these? Evidently they were unable to climb, or they would have followed him ere this. The fact that they did not leave, even after several more hours had elapsed, made it evident that they expected to get him.

He had been hearing a peculiar crunching sound some time before he located it and guessed the terrible truth.

They were gnawing through the base of the tree trunk!

When morning came, it looked as if Grandon's luck was running out. He'd made a desperate leap when the first tree started to fall and landed on another. The beasts followed and started to work on his new refuge. He'd found what felt like a coarse thick rope, and recognized it as the stem of one of the large climbing ferns he'd seen the day before. That led him to the crown of another tree twice the size of the one he left. But now the beasts had felled that one and were patiently gnawing at his third refuge.

Now he could see them below — twelve of the most fearsome creatures he'd ever seen. They looked like hyenas, but were twice as large, their bodies covered with thick scales, black and mottled with orange spots. Each beast had three horns, one projecting from either temple, and one sprouting between the eyes. Six of them were gnawing at the base of his tree while the other six rested. Apparently they were working in shifts.

Then he saw a man about two hundred yards away, walking with his eyes on the ground as if following a trail. He was armed with scarbo, tork, and knife, and carried a long bundle strapped to his back. Someone sent out to trail the fugitive slave, no doubt, Grandon thought. Well, he'd have a surprise soon.

A moment later, one of the beasts scented the newcomer, and uttered the laugh with which Grandon was now familiar. All work on Grandon's tree stopped and the pack charged the stranger.

Now the Earthman witnessed the power of the tork. The leader of the pack fell a full fifty feet from his quarry; seven more met a similar fate in as many seconds. The rest turned and fled. Then the man drew his knife and coolly and deliberately cut the throat of each animal. He glanced at the two fallen trees, then walked over to the one in which Grandon was perched.

"Come down, Robert Grandon," he said, in English.

Grandon was so surprised he nearly fell out of the tree.

"Who are you," he asked, "and where did you learn my language?"

"Come down and I will explain."

"You might come up," suggested Grandon. "I don't fancy the climate down there. I suppose you have instructions to bring me back dead or alive. I won't go back alive."

"You are mistaken, Robert Grandon. I have come to your aid. To prove this, I need only mention that I have communicated with Dr. Morgan of your planet for several years. Now will you come?"

Grandon slid down the rough tree trunk. When he reached the ground, the stranger advanced. "Permit me to introduce myself. I am Vorn Vangal, and my home is in the distant country of Olba."

"How do you do, Mr. Vangal," replied Grandon, extending his hand.

Vorn Vangal looked puzzled. "What is it you wish?"

"Why — nothing at all. I forgot that our custom of shaking hands might be unknown here."

"I have never heard of it," said Vangal. "I hope you will pardon the ignorance which kept me from returning your proffered salute. Show me how you do it, please."

Grandon explained, and for the first time in the history of that planet, two men shook hands on Zarovia.

"A very pretty custom," Vangal said. "I shall introduce it in Olba on my return. I will explain the various forms of salutes used on Zarovia. When one is presented to a stranger he merely bows slightly and acknowledges with words. Two intimate friends on meeting sometimes press their foreheads together. Then there are the military salutes, the salutes to royalty, *et cetera*. For instance, the reigning Torrogina of Reabon — or princess as you would call her — would be saluted thus." He made a low bow and extended his hand as Grandon had seen the slaves do the day before in front of the shrine.

"In the company with my fellow slaves, I bowed thus before a picture of a beautiful young woman yesterday," said Grandon. "Can it be that this is the Amazon princess of whom Dr. Morgan spoke?"

"She can be none other than Vernia, Princess of Reabon, who has ruled that country since the death of her father, Margo, who made Reabon the largest and mightiest empire in all Zarovia."

"I should like to meet her," said Grandon.

"To say that you should like to meet her is equivalent to saying that you should like to die. Thaddor, Prince of Uxpo, whose body you now inhabit on Zarovia, had the temerity to make love to her. She sentenced him to work in the quarries for life; and to run away after such a sentence has been passed in equivalent to signing your own death warrant, in Reabon."

"Nevertheless, I hope some day to meet her. By the way, friend Vangal, I suspect that you have food and drink in that long bundle you are carrying, and I have tasted neither since yesterday morning."

"Can it be possible?" ejaculated Vangal. "But of course! You are not familiar with the fern forest of Zarovia. No one carries food or drink in these forests, for both are about him in abundance."

He drew his knife and cut a branch from the bush-fern under which they were standing. "Here. Taste water as pure and delicious as may be found on Zarovia."

Grandon put the end of the branch to his lips and drank greedily, while Vangal gathered several large spore-pods and split them open with his knife.

"I shall have to teach you the woodcraft of Zarovia before I leave you," said Vangal. "But come, we must go as far as possible from this vicinity at once, or the soldiers of the Torrogina may find us."

"I am puzzled to know how it happened that you found me before the Reabonians," said Grandon.

"Because I followed your trail, while they merely ran about in the forest, guessing at what direction you had taken. The men of Reabon know nothing of following a trail, which is as an open book to my people of Olba. But here, I have brought you weapons and trappings." Vangal unrolled the long bundle. "Fasten this belt about your waist and cross the straps over your shoulders, so. Now let us be off."

The two swung away through the forest glades, Grandon armed like his companion with tork, scarbo and knife. As they walked side by side, Vangal explained the use of the tork, and showed Grandon how to insert the extra clips of bullets and gas which were in his belt.

"What do you call those strange creatures that treed me last night, and why did you cut their throats after you had already dispatched them with bullets?" inquired Grandon.

"They are called hahoes, so named because of their peculiar cries, and are mostly eaters of carrion, although they will seek and bring down fresh meat when driven to do so by hunger. I cut their throats because the poison in the tork bullets paralyzes temporarily, but does not kill. I prefer to use this kind rather than those bullets which carry deadly poison."

The sun was high in the heavens when they reached the bank of a small stream. Here the character of the vegetation changed considerably, for while large tree-ferns were still in evidence here and there, as well as the smaller varieties, there were huge fungus growing unlike anything Grandon had previously encountered. Colossal toadstools, some of which reared their heads for fifty feet in the air, grew all about in an endless variety of forms and colors.

"We are now more than twenty miles from the marble quarries and in an excellent place for a camp," said Vangal. "I will help you build a shelter and remain with you for a week to teach you Zarovian woodcraft, and patoa. At the end of that time I must journey to the other side of the planet in order to assist your friend, Harry Thorne."

"What is patoa?" asked Grandon.

"It is the universal language of Zarovia," replied Vangal. "While every nation has its own language, we have, in addition, patoa, which is taught to the children of every country from infancy. When you have mastered the tongue, you will have the means of conversing with any intelligent being you may meet."

The rest of the day was spent in building Grandon's new abode.

CHAPTER IV

After they had eaten on the following morning, Vorn Vangal said: "No doubt you are anxious to know something about this country, and the person you represent on Zarovia. The wild, mountainous kingdom of Uxpo, of which these forests are a part, is situated at the extreme southern limit of the empire of Reabon. Uxpo, together with seven other kingdoms, was originally conquered by the famous emperor, Margo, and its fierce, previously unbeaten mountaineer people reduced to slavery.

"Upon Margo's death, three years ago, the people of Uxpo entertained high hopes of freedom. They had learned that the emperor's daughter, Vernia, a mere slip of a girl, had succeeded to the throne; they revolted and, almost overnight, slew every soldier, officer and agent of the empire. Their old kin had been executed by Margo at the time of the invasion, but his elder son, Lugi, was placed on the throne.

"Two days afterward a courier brought news that the princess Vernia was coming at the head of a hundred thousand soldiers. Lugi assembled his five thousand mountaineers and went forth. They army of Uxpo was annihilated, and Lugi was executed for treason. Once more the fierce Uxponians bowed their necks to the yoke of the conqueror.

"Lugi had a young brother named Thaddor — your double. This youth was of a mild and gentle disposition, and it was for this reason, perhaps, that Vernia spared his life and allowed him the privilege of her court.

"Prince Thaddor, however, fell madly in love with her. He had always found women susceptible to him; so when one evening he attempted to make love to her, he was little prepared for the storm of anger which followed, and his being condemned to labor in the quarries for life.

"For some time I have been searching for a man dissatisfied with life on this planet, to accompany our Prince of Olba on the journey to your world. I heard of Prince Thaddor's predicament, and experienced little difficulty in persuading him. When Dr. Morgan reported that you were about to make the journey I immediately came hither in order to be of assistance to you. On learning you escaped, I trailed you to the tree in which you had been driven by the hahoes. The rest you know."

Vangal stayed with Grandon for a week, teaching him patoa and woodcraft, and the use of the tork and scarbo. On the evening of the seventh day he stated that the time had arrived for him to return.

"No doubt you are anxious to be back among your friends," remarked Grandon. "Is this journey a long one?"

"Olba is on the opposite side of the planet; roughly about twelve thousand of your Earth miles from here."

"And you will go all that distance on foot?"

"Hardly. My airship is concealed in a ravine only a short distance from here. In one day's time I shall be home. By leaving here in the evening I shall arrive there in the morning, for it is morning in Olba when it is evening in Reabon."

"What motive power do you use?"

"Ah, my friend, I regret that I am not at liberty to divulge that, for Olba is the only country on the planet in which airships are made or used. The factories and the secrets of manufacture are the exclusive property of the government, and have been since the first airship was invented, nearly four thousand centuries ago.

"My people are not given to conquest. In the airship they have a potent means of defense from their warlike neighbors. If the Reabonians, for example, knew the secret, they would long ago have subjugated most of the other Zarovian nations."

Together the men walked to the ravine where the airship was concealed. Grandon beheld what looked like a small metal duck-boat with a curved glass dome over the tiny cockpit. The airship was about ten feet long and three wide, and without planes, wings, propeller or rudder.

Vangal noted the look of surprise on the face of his companion.

"You seem puzzled," he said, smiling slightly. "It will do no harm for me to explain something of this craft's general principles, so long as I do not betray the actual secret of motive power.

"Immediately in front of the glass dome you will notice a small, round bulge in the deck. Under the bulge is a delicate mechanism which it is impossible to remove or take apart without breaking a small vial of acid that will instantly destroy it. This mechanism is the motive power of the craft, so you can readily see that it would be quite impossible for an enemy to learn our secret by capturing one of our ships.

"You have heard of telekinesis — the power with which your terrestrial mediums sometimes cause tables and other ponderable objects to rise and hang suspended, or move about in the air without physical aid. My people have been familiar with this wonderful power of the mind for many centuries; this mechanism responds to, and amplifies telekinesis to a remarkable degree. By mind power I am able to cause the ship to rise and hang suspended at almost any altitude, or to move in any direction, backward, forward, or sidewise. For emergency use, in the event of the failure of the motive power, there are two parachutes, one under the small round lid at either end of the craft. By pressing a button I cause the lids to fly back and the parachutes to project from the holes and open almost instantly."

"A most astounding and wonderful invention," exclaimed Grandon.

"Perhaps some day you will visit Olba, and when you do, Vorn Vangal will see that you are provided with a suitable craft as long as you stay in the country — for none but a government official or employee may take one of these airships over the border. It is growing late, and I must begin my journey," Vangal continued, opening the door in the rear of the dome and stepping inside. "Farewell, my friend. I admonish you to hurry home at once. I see you have not brought your tork or scarbo with you. On Zarovia you are in constant danger from attack by man or beast. Farewell, and may you soon be settled on the throne of Uxpo."

Grandon warmly clasped the hand of his departing friend, and a feeling of indefinable sadness came over him as he watched the tiny craft rise noiselessly and smoothly to the height of perhaps a thousand feet, then dart away, to be lost to view in a few seconds.

As he stood looking in the direction Vangal had taken, he was startled by the sound of a stealthy footfall behind him. He wheeled, but his eyes could not penetrate the shadows, for night had come on with its characteristic suddenness. At the sound of a second footfall he turned and dashed off through the forest, only to find himself amid a group of warriors with leveled torks.

CHAPTER V

Despite the fact that the audience chamber of the imperial palace of Reabon was crowded with people, the silence was intense, for the scarlet curtains which surrounded the massive throne had been drawn back, signifying the approach of the Torrogina.

Those who stood at the lower end of the hall and farthest from the throne were the slaves, the prevailing color of whose garments were gray. Next to the slaves stood the common people — tradesmen, farmers, merchants, mechanics, and the like — attired in blue. Then came the nobles and their families, who might be recognized anywhere by their purple garments; and finally members of the royal families of Reabon and her many rogats, who were privileged to wear scarlet, the universal Zarovian color of royalty, and to stand next to the throne during audiences.

All eyes were turned toward the door as four men entered, carrying the great golden palanquin with curtains of scarlet. The litter-bearers all wore heavy beards, cut off square below their chin. On their heads were jeweled golden crowns, and their scarlet garments proclaimed their royal birth. They were kings of four of the sixteen kingdoms which comprised the empire of Reabon, and were serving their allotted time in attendance on the Torrogina Vernia, as was required by law.

Behind the palanquin walked the illustrious Orthad, commander of all the armies of Reabon, and responsible to the princess herself. He was armed with tork and scarbo, and resplendent in his magnificent uniform, which was of purple, decorated with no inconsiderable quantity of gold fringe, gold braid and jewels. On a scarlet cushion held before him he carried the great jeweled scarbo, scepter of Reabonian authority.

A hundred members of the Imperial Guard marched behind in double file, and ranged themselves at regular intervals along the wall. Their uniforms were of an olive green color, decorated with silver in lieu of gold which adorned that of their commander.

When the four palanquin-bearers arrived at the foot of the throne which was reached by four broad steps, they gently lowered their burden to the floor, and each stepped forward and lay, face downward, on one of the steps. No sooner had they taken their places than the scarlet curtains parted, and the beautiful ruler of the greatest empire in all Zarovia, Vernia of Reabon, emerged and ascended the four human steps to the throne.

As she took her seat with quiet dignity, everyone bowed low

with right hand extended palm downward. She sat there attired in a clinging garment of scarlet material that left her white arms and shoulders bare, her jeweled crown resting lightly on her fluffy golden curls.

The first person to seek audience before the throne was a gaily-uniformed ambassador from the great western empire of Mernerum, laden with costly presents, and bringing a proposal of marriage, despite the fact that this same suitor had been refused a score of times before.

When Bonal, her prime minister, advised her that the ambassador from Mernerum sought audience, Vernia looked a trifle bored. "Are there not several other ambassadors with presents and similar messages waiting without?" she asked.

"Yes, your majesty, there are ten in all from as many empires."

"Send them all in at once. I can say 'No' to all collectively; otherwise our entire day will be taken up and important business of the empire will have to be postponed."

The ten ambassadors, each followed by a concourse of slaves laden with the most costly presents a great emperor could procure, and humbly bowed before the throne. Bonal announced their ten proposals as one. Vernia promptly and courteously declined, and they sadly took their departure.

Her matrimonial offers disposed of, the Torrogina listened to the reports of the rulers of her various provinces. Last on the list came Uxpo, as it was the last kingdom conquered. Though the other provinces were ruled by princes, this one was under the control of a military commander; its people had not been completely subjugated. A captain bore tidings from his commander. He humbly approached the foot of the throne, waited for permission to speak, then announced: "Prince Thaddor has escaped from the quarries. He nearly killed two of his guards and ran away into the fern forest."

Vernia was greatly surprised. That Prince Thaddor had found courage to escape seemed incredible to her; but that he had nearly killed two of his guards in the process seemed little short of miraculous.

"You have sent soldiers after him, I presume."

"Men are scouring the forests and mountains in search of him, but up to the time of my departure, no trace had been found. There is another matter of which my commander bids me speak. It has been prophesied by some unknown soothsayer that a great fighter is coming from another world to lead Uxpo to victory and independence. This ridiculous prediction has spread throughout the kingdom, and as a result it is seething with unrest. The Fighting Traveks of Uxpo make nightly raids on our soldiers, and even the women and children have grown rebellious."

Vernia frowned slightly. "This mutiny must be put down, once and for all. Orthad: assemble an army of ten thousand men at once — I will lead them in person. Bonal: my palanquin-bearers. Postpone all further hearings until my return from Uxpo."

A half hour later two men stood on one of the smaller balconies of the imperial palace in whispered conversation. One wore the scarlet of royalty, the other the purple of the nobility and the trappings and insignia of an imperial commander.

The one in scarlet, a youth of twenty, whispered hoarsely: "Have a care, my worthy Zueppa. I hear quite well, you know. Are you sure the four men who are to constitute her personal bodyguard will not fail us?"

"Their loyalty to your highness, Prince Destho, is beyond question. If they fail they will die, rather than betray us."

"They must not fail. After all, the task is not too difficult. They have only to hide her in the northern mountains for a year — a short year, mind you — then none will dare to question my title to the throne. And you, my faithful Zueppa: Second only to myself, you will hold the greatest office in Zarovia."

"May I not again remind your highness that there is a much easier and simpler way to attain our ends?"

"Stop, fool! Do you take me for an assassin? My ambition is great, but my desire for this woman is greater. You must detain her for a year; then return her to me unharmed."

Within half an hour of his capture by these men who called themselves the Fighting Traveks, Robert Ellsmore Grandon learned how quickly a man's status could change in Zarovia. They were impressed by the fact that he wore the color of royalty and seemed baffled when he identified himself as Grandon of Earth.

After a brief consultation amongst themselves, the stranger was given a choice. He could go his way in peace, or remain with the Fighting Traveks once he demonstrated his fitness — which meant overcoming whichever of them he chose to encounter in a duel. Since the alternative would be to face the Venusian beasts alone and unarmed, Grandon challenged the leader of this band.

The man was a good fighter, but the art of fencing was unknown here. Once Grandon adjusted himself to the scarbo, and his opponent's manner of fighting — which was roughly comparable to scimitar or broadsword technique — a well-directed lunge stretched the leader of the Fighting Traveks at the Earthman's feet.

Then came the surprise. The band now greeted Grandon as their mojak; he had beaten the leader — he was now in command. When his second-in-command came up for orders, Grandon told him to carry on as before.

The lieutenant saluted. "Did you say your name was Grandon of Urgg? I cannot pronounce it."

"Well, you may call me Grandon of Terra," he suggested.

"Grandon of Terra!" the lieutenant repeated. "We salute you."

The men prepared shelter and the evening meal; soon after, all retired. Grandon drifted off to slumber with difficulty, still marveling at the swift events; it seemed that he had slept but a moment or two when a deafening din assailed his ears. All about him men were fighting, cursing, shouting, and groaning.

"What is up?" he asked the man nearest him.

"It is the Reabonians," replied the man, stanching the blood from a cut in his shoulder. "We are surrounded by the soldiers of the princess."

CHAPTER VI

The instant Grandon learned they were being attacked by Reabonians, he was on his feet directing the fighting. First at one point, then another, he momentarily filled a gap where a man had been cut down. The little circle of Traveks was narrowing swiftly. They fought bravely, but the odds were in favor of the Reabonians.

The battle cry of the attackers was "For Vernia, for Vernia!"

"For Grandon of Terra!" answered the Traveks, defiantly.

Suddenly a cry came from one of the leaders of the Reabonians. "Truce!"

Instantly the fighting ceased. Grandon's men lowered their weapons as the soldiers of Vernia withdrew a little way.

"Where is your captain?" shouted the Reabonian commander.

"Here," replied Grandon.

"I offer you the alternative of surrender or complete annihilation, Grandon of Terra," said the officer. "Two-thirds of your company lie bleeding on the ground. You can save the others from a like fate by laying down your arms."

"What say you, men?" asked Grandon, looking around.

"We are Fighting Traveks!"

A surge of pride swept over him. If there were only some way — he racked his brain for a feasible plan. Like a flash there came to his mind a vision of old football days. He lowered his voice and issued a few swift orders. The men formed a circle once more, and Grandon shouted defiance to the Reabonian commander.

The fighting had all taken place by the flickering light of the campfires. Each Travek, as he took up his position, pushed a quantity of loose moss before him with his feet. The soldiers of the princess were closing in on them when Grandon issued a sharp command. Simultaneously every fire was smothered under a heap of moss.

Another command, and the men had formed a flying wedge with Grandon at the apex. Straight through the circle of attackers they smashed in compact formation, cutting right and left. As they ran through the forest lanes they could hear the Reabonians fighting each other in the darkness.

When they had attained some little distance from the scene of battle the smoldering fire flared up once more, and they heard a shout of baffled rage go up from the Torrogina's men.

Grandon had laid down to sleep with a command of sixty-five men. They numbered now but nineteen, and the lieutenant was missing. Grandon turned to the man nearest him. "Are there other bands of Fighting Traveks nearby?"

"A number of them rove these woods, but as none tarry long in one place we might hope to find them only by accident. Bordeen, the great commander of all the bands, with three hundred men in a valley only twelve miles from here."

"Can you find the place tonight?"

"Unless we run into Reabonians."

"Then lead the way, and let us be off at once."

They were halted by a sentry at some distance from the camp; at a sign from the guide, they were allowed to proceed without interruption.

The camp consisted of a half dozen circular huts similar to the one Grandon's men had constructed, surrounding a much larger hut which he took to be the headquarters of the commander. The guide led him straight to this structure and, before he realized it, he found himself in the presence of Bordeen.

There was no light within the enclosure except the flickering rays cast by the campfires surrounding the camp, and Grandon could only imperfectly discern the features of Bordeen and those who stood about him.

The guide saluted with drawn scarbo held pointing at an angle of forty-five degrees, and the Earthman did likewise.

"Mightiest of commanders," the Travek said, "if it is your pleasure, our new captain, Grandon of Terra, will make his report."

"A new captain!" exclaimed Bordeen. "This is indeed strange. Thelpo was a mighty fighter. Report, Grandon of Terra."

Grandon modestly described the duel that followed his chance meeting with the Fighting Traveks, how they had been surrounded by a large body of Reabon soldiers and all but annihilated. He expected a reprimand for losing two-thirds of his command, but Bordeen commended his generalship in effecting an escape when escape seemed hopeless.

His report concluded, he was conducted to the hut where his men were quartered, and was soon asleep on his mossy couch. The guide, however, remained by order of the commander, who asked: "What know you of this Grandon of Terra?"

"Nothing he has not told you for himself, other than that he is from a far-distant country which he calls Terra, and is a most extraordinary fighter with the scarbo as well as an exceedingly able commander. No doubt you noticed that he wore the color of royalty."

"Hardly. In this dim light I cannot tell scarlet from any other color. I fear my eyes are failing me. However, it seemed to me as he stood there, that there was something strangely familiar about him."

A man at Bordeen's right spoke up. "Was it not of Prince Thaddor that he reminded you?"

"Yes — now that you mention it, he did. Could it be that cruel treatment has changed our gentle prince into a fighting man? . . . Bring me a flashlight. There is a mark on Prince Thaddor's foot that few knew of, and it could not be simulated. Should it be he, we must dispatch runners to gather in all our scattered bands, for then a great feast will be in order."

The long-suppressed hope in Bordeen's heart was making him plan before examining the evidence. But when he and the others emerged from the sleeping Grandon's shelter, there was no doubt in anyone's mind.

Grandon's awakening on the following morning was perhaps as much of a surprise as was the memorable morning when he first opened his eyes in the quarry-slaves' sleeping quarters.

The rude hut in which he slept had been draped with curtains of shimmering scarlet cloth, and the interior hung with wreaths, festoons and shields on which were emblazoned the coat of arms of the royal house of Uxpo. The men of his command, who had occupied the hut with him, now introduced themselves respectively as his valet and his armorer.

At first he thought some joke was being perpetrated by the commander, but was assured that this was not the case. He permitted his hair to be cut after the prevailing fashion of Uxpo, but when his valet commenced to trim his beard, which was cut off square below the chin, in accordance with the custom of the land, he demurred and ordered a clean shave.

As the armorer buckled a broad belt about him, from which descended a tork embossed with silver, and a scarbo whose hilt was gold set with jewels, he said: "As it is your duty to supply me with weapons, I am going to ask you to procure a sword for me."

"I will procure it for your highness if it be humanly possible, but I have never heard of one. If I might have a description, perhaps . . ."

"Of course you have never heard of it. It is a weapon used on another planet. Have your metal workers fashion a weapon with a hilt like a scarbo, but with a long, straight, two-edged blade, slender and pliable, and of the strongest tempered steel."

The armorer bowed with his hand extended palm downward, and backed through the doorway.

He had scarcely departed, ere Bordeen entered, followed by a concourse of Uxponian nobles and officers. All bowed low before Grandon in the customary salute to royalty.

Accepting their homage courteously, he permitted himself to be conducted to the head of a huge banquet table on which a sumptuous feast was spread, amid the ringing cheers of a thousand Fighting Traveks.

Bordeen made the formal speech of welcome, addressing Grandon as Prince Thaddor. Then the latter arose.

"Comrade," he began, "your mighty commander has just addressed me as Prince Thaddor. I have come among you to do the work of your prince, not to assume his name, for I am not Thaddor, nor is he any longer an inhabitant of this world. While he lives my life on the planet Earth — or Terra — it shall be my endeavor to lead you to victory. I therefore assume leadership of your armies, men of Uxpo, not as Prince Thaddor, but as Grandon of Terra."

This speech spread consternation in the ranks of the Fighting Traveks. As he resumed his seat there was no applause — only an ominous silence. Grandon resolved to tender his resignation, when Bordeen stood up, flushed with the fever of inspiration.

"My countrymen, a prophecy has been fulfilled. Some time ago I learned that a wise man, a prophet and seer from the distant land of Olba, was in this vicinity. In my extremity and worry I sought him out. This is what he told me:

"'Go back to your people and tell them to be of good cheer, for your royal leader will soon be with you. He will be young and strong, and expert with the scarbo, but his first request will be for a weapon which he calls a sword. He will resemble a prince of Uxpo who will have, by the time, journeyed to another world. Reject him and you will see him no more. Accept him, and he will lead you to victory.'"

There was a brief instant of awed silence as Bordeen finished his discourse. Then, as if by a prearranged signal, a thousand scarbos flashed on high and a thousand voices thundered: "Long live Grandon of Terra, Prince of Uxpo!"

Ere the tumult had ceased, the armorer threaded his way through the crowd, holding before him a scarlet cushion on which reposed a weapon new and strange to all Zarovians. He deposited it before Grandon, just as the tumult was subsiding.

Grandon drew it from its scabbard and held it aloft, saying: "This is the sword of which your prophet spoke. I pledge it with my life to the cause of Uxpo."

Grandon, exalted as he was, found time to marvel at the clever planning of Vorn Vangal — or whatever agent of Dr. Morgan's had put across this prophecy. Then a courier dashed breathlessly into the hall.

"The Reabonians!" he gasped. "They are coming, a great army of them, lead by the princess herself! We are hemmed in on three sides."

By this time more runners were arriving from different directions, all with descriptions of a mighty army encircling the camp.

Grandon marshaled his men for a retreat toward the north — the only direction left open to them — urging the utmost speed; for to have those converging wings meet ahead of them meant almost certain defeat.

As it was, they were barely in time for a swift charge between them under a heavy fire of tork bullets which exacted a heavy toll from their ranks. They were still far from safety, however, for the Reabonians followed in swift pursuit.

Grandon held council with Bordeen and they decided to make for a narrow mountain pass nearly four miles distant, which led to a valley beyond.

After a running fight lasting more than two hours, they reached their objective with their numbers sadly depleted. They had reckoned, however, without the military genius of Princess Vernia; she had anticipated this move and filled the narrow pass with armed men.

The Uxpo troops were in a trap from which escape seemed utterly impossible. The pass was out of the question, for with even a small body of men defending it, it was practically invulnerable. On either side of the entrance rose sheer precipices, which even a monkey-man could not have scaled, while in front of them there was an army of between eight and nine thousand men.

Grandon kept to the front ranks, shouting encouragement to his men, and using his sword to such good advantage that at times the Reabonians fell away from him in sheer wonder at his prowess.

But the Traveks were fighting a hopeless battle; already their number was reduced to less than five hundred.

At this juncture a force intervened on which neither of the contestants had counted. Grandon's first inkling of what was to take place was the sight of a mass of black clouds, apparently hanging midway between the tree-tops and those fleecy, silver-gray mists which are ever present in the upper Zarovian atmosphere, and moving swiftly toward them.

He had expected a storm, but when it burst in all its fury he was ill-prepared for such a violent demonstration of the power of the elements. The first torrent of rain was followed by inky darkness, punctuated at intervals by brilliant flashes of lightning. The thunder roared incessantly, reverberating through the mountains, and fighting, either by sound or sight, was made exceedingly difficult.

It was Grandon's opportunity to save what remained of his little army, and he was not slow to take advantage of it. He called Bordeen to his side.

"Make haste and divide the command into small parties of not more than twenty men each," he said. "In the confusion of the storm, small bodies of men can escape with little or no fighting, whereas a charge by the entire company would be sure to be detected and opposed every foot of the way. Tonight each band must shift for itself; tomorrow we will reunite. The place of rendezvous will be the base of those great twin mountains which mark the northernmost end of this valley."

As Bordeen hastened away to carry out the plans, his commander once more took his place in the line of battle, forging steadily ahead.

It was some time before he discovered that his comrades were no longer with him. Then a particularly brilliant flash of lightning revealed the fact that he was completely surrounded by enemy soldiers. They saw his plight at the same instant, and rushed at him in the darkness that followed. Acting on a sudden thought, he turned swiftly about, and facing in the opposite direction, walked slowly backward.

The ruse worked, for the men behind him, believing him to be one of their comrades who was a little timid about approaching the great swordsman, surged around and ahead of him. When the last man had passed he turned once more, and ran for the forest.

What troubled him most was how to gauge his course through the dense, dripping labyrinth that engulfed him.

At this juncture he heard a noise as of a small body of men running ahead of him; he decided to follow them as swiftly and silently as possible, and make sure they were not Reabonians before divulging his presence.

As the minutes wore on, he could tell by the sounds ahead that he was gaining. Suddenly he emerged from the forest and found himself on a flat, sandy beach. A flash of lightning revealed the fact that he was not following a body of men, but a huge reptile, a gigantic amphibian with a monstrous lizard-like body to which was attached a serpentine head and neck of immense proportions. It was pursuing someone else with an agility little short of marvelous for so ponderous a body, and had almost come up with its quarry.

The victim, who appeared little more than a slender boy, was making frantic efforts to escape, but it appeared that his doom was inevitable.

Another lightning flash showed the reptile with neck arched and jaws distended, ready to strike. A cry of mortal terror came to him from the darkness. Grandon unsheathed his sword.

CHAPTER VII

It was only because there came so swift a lull in the storm that Grandon was able to follow the monster to its subterranean cave. The big reptile crouched with its back toward him as he came upon it, its body half out of the water.

On the floor lay its victim, but the creature seemed to be in no hurry. It was nosing its prey, in the manner of a cat playing with a mouse. Presently, the victim sat up, rubbing his eyes.

Grandon raised the muzzle of his tork above the water, aimed for the swaying head, and touched the button. At the sound and impact, the creature turned — and Grandon was dealt a blow from behind that hurled him into the far corner of the cave.

The tork bullets were useless; he drew his sword as he dodged about in the cave to elude snapping jaws and that scaly tail which had floored him before. It seemed hopeless; his point glanced off the creature's scales as from armor plate.

Cornered, those jaws open to seize him, he lunged out wildly. The weapon was jerked from his hand, but no teeth closed upon him. Then he saw that he had driven his blade through the reptile's eyes and deep into its brain. After a few shudders, it keeled over.

Bracing his foot against the massive head, he wrenched his sword free, and turned to face the youth who was approaching him. "Come," he said, "we must get out of here quickly." Another creature might appear, and Grandon didn't want to trust to luck again.

A dim light emanated from a point farther back. There was a small hole in the top of the bank, and Grandon widened it with his sword, enough to let them through.

Outside, the Earthman had a chance really to observe his companion, who was clad from head to foot in shining scarlet leather. The head and face were covered by a pointed hood of the same material; on impulse, Grandon reached forward and pulled back the concealing headpiece. That was when he gasped in wonder.

For a moment, the golden-haired girl thus revealed met his astonished gaze; then she regained her poise, with a look of regal hauteur. "Why did you do that?" she asked icily.

"Frankly, I do not know. If I have offended, I crave your pardon."

Some of the coldness departed, but she did not smile. "Then let us be on our way," she said, adjusting her hood.

He turned and, together, they walked back among the lengthening shadows toward the river's edge. Owing to the recent cloudburst the current was abnormally swift, carrying the floating storm debris past them at express-train speed. There were great, uprooted trees, detached branches and leaves of various sizes and kinds, and a number of huge toadstools.

As they stood there on the brink, the cap of a great orange-colored toadstool was caught in an eddy and whirled against the shore. The stem had been broken off completely, and it formed a watertight basin about twelve feet in diameter. Grandon leaped forward and hauled it in.

"What are you going to do with that?" asked the girl.

"If I can cut a suitable paddle," replied Grandon, "I believe I can make it serve as a boat to convey us across the river, where I have reason to suspect your friends, as well as mine, are located."

He looked about until he found a strong branch that suited his purpose, then made a most serviceable paddle by using the limb for the handle and the base of the broad leaf for the blade.

"Come," said Grandon. "We must start quickly if we would gain the other shore before dark."

She stepped aboard, and Grandon pushed off, wading out to where the water was breast-deep before climbing up beside her in order to clear the eddy which might again carry the craft shoreward.

The Earthman had taken many canoe trips, but he had not considered the difference in shape between a canoe and the inverted cap of a Zarovian toadstool. Instead of making the headway he anticipated, he found himself merely going around in a circle.

It was some time before he found a way simultaneously to guide and propel his awkward craft, which he accomplished by standing on the side toward which he wished to go and scooping the water toward him. They laboriously reached midstream after about an hour's hard paddling, but in the interim the swift current had carried them many miles from their starting point. Then, to Grandon's consternation, the paddle broke.

"I guess we're in for in now," he said dejectedly. "Fool that I was to risk your life in this overgrown bowl."

"What of your own life?" she replied. "You are running no less risk than I."

As she spoke darkness descended, the black, moonless darkness of Venus. Grandon sat in moody silence, straining his eyes in his effort to penetrate the surrounding gloom, his ears on the alert for any sound which might indicate the presence of the dangerous reptilian creatures that inhabited the waters.

Presently a soft hand sought his, and clung there.

"What is it?" he asked hoarsely, endeavoring to still the quiver of emotion that suddenly took possession of his vocal cords.

"I am tired — oh, so tired. And yes, frightened. To think that *I* should be frightened!"

"Here," he said, stripping off his cloak and rolling it into a pillow. "I have been inexcusably thoughtless. Now lie with your head on this pillow, so, and try to get some sleep. I will keep watch."

He withdrew a little way and once more sat quietly with senses alert for the slightest sound or sign of hostile attack. It was some time before her regular breathing, scarcely audible above the sound of the rushing waters, told him that she slept.

Toward morning the noises made by the amphibians ceased, and Grandon grew drowsy. His head nodded forward on his breast. Suddenly their craft gave a terrific lurch that rolled the girl into his lap. It was only his clutching the gills of the toadstool with both hands that kept them from being pitched into the water.

"What was that?" asked the girl, breathlessly, awake in an instant.

Another lurch followed.

"Hold on and I will try to find out," he said.

Drawing his sword, he crept near the edge while the lurching continued. He clung to the rim with one hand and prodded the water about him with his sword, completely circling the craft without encountering anything other than the rushing water. It was not until a dash of spray struck him in the face and he tasted salt that he realized the truth. They were on a body of salt water, possibly a large lake or an ocean. He made his way back to where the girl clung, and related his discovery.

"The river on which we were floating," she explained, "empties into the great Azpok Ocean, the ocean of mysteries, of man-eating monsters and of terrible storms that destroy the mightiest of ships as easily as the smallest boats. To navigate the ocean is to court death in many sudden and appalling forms."

An hour passed before morning dawned. In the meantime the roughness of the sea had abated a little, making it less difficult to keep their places. They were riding long, rolling swells that elevated and lowered their craft with very little lurching. There was no land in sight.

All through that long, sultry day and the following night they drifted, without sighting aught save birds and a few leaping fish. Just before dawn they were rudely startled by a violent tilting of their craft, followed by a roaring and swirling of the water about them. Grandon barely had time to seize the girl ere they were engulfed by a huge wave which capsized the craft and precipitated them into a seething maelstrom of black water.

Down — down, they went into the dark depth. The Earthman fought gamely, but as the minutes passed the violence of the waves increased and he felt his strength waning. He realized that, barring the intervention of some unforeseen aid, the battle against death would soon end in defeat.

With body numbed and hope gone, he suddenly felt the sandy beach below his feet. He staggered forward, dragging the girl with him, and was knocked flat by a mighty breaker. Crawling painfully onward, driving his flagging muscles by a supreme effort of will, he finally collapsed on the dry sand, just beyond reach of the waves.

When Grandon regained consciousness it was daylight. His first thought was for the girl who lay face downward beside him. As he lifted her tenderly in his arms he gave silent thanks, for she was breathing.

Presently she opened her eyes and, for a moment, there was a startled expression in them. "Where are we?" she asked.

"I haven't the slightest idea," replied Grandon. "I have no knowledge of Zarovian geography."

"A prince, and you know naught of geography? That is indeed strange. Do they not teach it in your country?"

"I am fairly well acquainted with the geography of the planet Earth — Terra — on which I was born, but we of that world know nothing of the geography of this one because of your cloud-filled atmosphere."

She looked up at him in amazement. "But you wear the garments and insignia of the royal house of Uxpo. Moreover, you very closely resemble a prince of that house. Who are you?"

"I am Robert Grandon, of Terra."

"Grandon, of Terra? Ah, I recall the name. A Grandon of Terra was recently acclaimed Prince of Uxpo. It was said that he came in fulfillment of a prophecy from another world. And you are he. Truly the pranks of fortune are most amazing! Yesterday I made war on you; today I look to you for protection."

"You made war on me? May I ask who you are?"

"Can it be that you do not recognize me? I am Vernia, of Reabon."

It all came to him in a flash. The lifelike painting in the shrine at the marble quarries . . .

"How did you happened to be wandering alone and unarmed in the fern forest?"

"I did not set out alone. When I started away from the camp I was accompanied by my four guards, and was armed with a tork and scarbo. Zueppa sent a messenger from the front to inform me that your men had broken through our lines and were headed for the camp. He advised me to leave at once, saying that the guards would conduct me to a safe place until your army had been overcome. I followed Zueppa's counsel, but had gone only a short distance when the guards disarmed me, and informed me that I was their prisoner.

"They were about to bind my hands when the giant reptile appeared on the scene. Though traitors they were brave men, for they stood their ground to do battle with the monster. He killed the foremost man with a single snap of his jaws. A second man met a like fate, and I believe he devoured all four of them — although I am not certain, as I turned and ran through the forest. When the storm came, I lost my bearings completely. I reached the river's edge and I fainted when I saw those terrible jaws poised above me. I presume that I should have been devoured then and there had the reptile not already eaten my guards."

"Who is Zueppa?"

"He is one of my officers — a good commander and strategist."

"He may be a good soldier, but he is unquestionably a liar. My men did not break through your lines at all until after the storm had struck, and then only in small, scattered groups."

"Then Zueppa was implicated in the plot. But who could have planned it, and for what purpose?"

"That, I am unable to tell you."

He looked at her so long and so searchingly that she grew uneasy. "Of what are you thinking?"

"I was wondering what fate you would have meted out to me had your men captured me yesterday."

She smiled. "I should probably have had you beheaded."

"And now . . ."

"If we reach Reabon in safety I shall make you supreme commander over all the armies."

"Why?"

"As your reward for saving my life."

"I ask no reward for that, nor could accept it, much as I appreciate the honor."

"It is the second highest in the greatest nation of Zarovia, an office second only to my own. Why, any king on the globe would be glad to exchange his position for it."

"I have been made Prince of Uxpo," replied Grandon, "under

my own name and because of my deeds in behalf of that kingdom. I should rather be the tiniest twinkling star in the heaven than the most beautiful and brilliant planet."

"I'm afraid I don't quiet understand."

"Planets shine by reflected light — stars by virtue of their own brilliancy. As your general I should merely reflect the greatness that is yours."

"Perhaps you should prefer to continue the war."

"Infinitely. But pray, let us hold to our truce. Until we can reach the safety of our own countries we are allies, you know."

"Rather, I am your prisoner of war . . . We talk much and get nowhere," she said wearily. "I am both hungry and thirsty. Do you not feed your prisoners of war?"

They walked inland through barren country to the foot of a lofty perpendicular cliff. Through a narrow fissure they caught a glimpse of greenery beyond, so they hurried between the frowning rock walls and at last emerged on level ground.

They were on the border of a small inland lake, the water of which was as clear as crystal. Ferns, mosses and fungi grew all about its borders in luxurious profusion, but what aroused Grandon's interest and curiosity most was the appearance of the bottom of the lake, which was plainly visible.

It was covered with hundreds of odd, grotesque growths — upright fluted columns with thick branches of the same pattern curving upward from the trunks like the arms of candelabra. On the tips of the branches were great clusters of brilliantly-hued fruit-like globes in an endless variety of form and color. The effect of the entire lake bottom was like that of a thousand rainbows fused into one.

A look of terror came into the eyes of the girl.

"Now I know only too well where we are," she said. "This must be one of the submarine gardens of the terrible flying grampites. I have heard some of our hardiest mariners tell of these gardens and the horrible creatures who guard them."

"Let us eat and drink, first, then talk of the grampites afterward," said Grandon. "They may be dangerous creatures, but they will have to go some to outclass that reptile."

A clear, cold spring, bubbling from the rock wall, satisfied their thirst, after which Grandon cut some spore-pods from a nearby fern and split them with his knife. They were in prime condition, and made a most pleasing meal for the famished wayfarers.

"It must be," Grandon remarked, "that these underwater fruits are especially delectable morsels, if men risk their lives for them."

"They are, and of a flavor that excels anything else that growns on Zarovia."

"I will gather some for you," said Grandon, removing his heavy trappings. "They should be easily plucked."

"No, no!" she cried. "Please don't go. You may be seen and killed by the grampites."

He laughed at her fears, and stripped down to his loincloth. Then, taking his long knife between his teeth, he plunged into the clear water, Swimming from cluster to cluster he found one that suited his fancy, and cut the thick stem.

As he did so, he saw a black shadow move swiftly across the surface of the lake above him. It puzzled him not a little, for he had seen no living creature other than his companion when he entered the water. He reached the surface with a few powerful strokes, and made for the point where he had left the girl, but the spot was deserted.

Vernia had disappeared as completely and mysteriously as if the earth had opened and swallowed her.

CHAPTER VIII

Cursing the foolhardiness that led him to leave the girl unguarded, Grandon hurled the fatal cluster of fruit far out into the lake. He found his clothing and weapons intact and dressed quickly. He had no sooner buckled on his sword and tork than a creature that surpassed in hideousness anything he had ever seen, swooped down on him.

Elevating the muzzle of his tork, he sent a stream of bullets at his assailant, and had the satisfaction of seeing it fall to the ground, where it fluttered for a moment, then lay still.

He examined it minutely and shuddered as he thought of the beautiful Vernia in the clutches of so loathsome a thing. The specimen he had brought down was about eight feet long from head to toe, and covered with a soft, mouse-colored fur.

Its head was shaped like that of a gorilla, but the ears were set high and were pointed like those of a fox. The nose was nothing more than a pair of flat, broad nostrils, set almost on a level with the eyes, and the mouth of a leech, being merely a round, puckered hole, whose sucker lips were furnished with tiny, razor-sharp protuberances.

The arms were fully as long as the body, and formed the framework for the membranous wings, the web of which stretched to the center of the back above the rear of the legs below, ending just above the heels. The trunk and lower limbs were shaped much like those of a man, the feet being most manlike in form, except that the five toes on each foot were armed with strong, up-curling claws.

Drawing his knife, he bent to cut the furry throat. Then something landed on his back with considerable force, two long, bony arms wound tightly about him, and he felt a sharp pain at the back on his neck as a sucker mouth gripped and lacerated his flesh.

He could not, in this position, use his sword or tork, but he gripped his knife firmly and plunged it again and again into the thing on his back, though with no apparent effect, for it hung on like the fabled old man of the sea. At last he found a vital spot, and the iron grip of the arms relaxed. As the creature fell away from him the lips tore loose with a pop like that of a champagne cork.

For a moment he imagined the attack was over, but five of the monsters now came hurtling at him from all directions. He fired his tork as they approached, and one fell in the lake, where it floated, looking at a distance much like an old broken umbrella. The foremost grampite did not alight on him as the other had done; it swooped straight toward him, head on, then rose slightly and raked him with its sharp upcurved claws.

His shoulder was bleeding profusely from the onslaught when the second attacker arrived, but this time Grandon was prepared. Leaping lightly to one side he plunged his sword into the furry body. The last two wheeled and joined the leader, now circling high above Grandon. Evidently they decided to go for reinforcements, for they turned suddenly and flew straight across the lake in the direction from which they had come.

Grandon marked their course, and noted that they flew straight toward a distant mountain peak from which a wisp of smoke lazily ascended. If Vernia had been carried off by grampites, this was the direction in which they must have taken her.

He walked around the rim of the lake, cut through the surrounding tree ferns and emerged on a broad, rolling plain that was covered with a carpet of resilient moss. Several hours were consumed in crossing the plain, then he came to another fern forest.

A short walk brought him abruptly to the edge of a small, crystalline lake, similar to the one he had just left. Instantly he leaped back in the shadow of the trees, for the place was literally alive with grampites. They were apparently engaged in harvesting the underwater fruit, and he watched the process with interest.

Skirting the lake with great care, he again pressed forward toward his smoking guidepost. He dodged and circled several more grampite-infested lakes. Then he came to a chain of low-lying, rocky hills that were without vegetation of any kind.

As he clambered over the jagged rocks, he noted a pungent odor in the air like that of sulfur, or perhaps some sulphurous compound. The atmosphere grew warmer and warmer until the heat was almost unbearable, and the acrid odor stung his nostrils and smarted his lungs. The rocks over which he scrambled now took on a uniform greenish-yellow hue.

Several times Grandon had wondered why these flying monsters had not been exterminated by the soldiers of the princess. He learned the reason as he brought up at the edge of a body of boiling water more than half a mile in width, and stretching in a broad, sweeping curve to his right and left. From this caldron rose greenish-yellow vapor, which would have asphyxiated anyone attempting to cross in a boat.

The huge mountain was in plain view now, its peak less than a mile away. Myraids of grampites swarmed about the summit.

Some of the incoming messengers were laden with fruit, others with the bodies of animals; and one, which flew over Grandon's head, carried the limp form of a sailor, its talons hooked through his belt. Grandon aimed his tork and was about to press the button, when the thought came that perhaps the man still lived, and a shot would precipitate both victim and captor into the bubbling, hissing sulfur lake.

As it was evident that he could not possibly cross the fuming barrier before him, he decided to follow the margin in the hope that he might find some means of ingress. Accordingly, he turned to the right, keeping just out of reach of the deadly vapors, and traveled as swiftly as the rugged character of the rocky formation would permit.

He had covered a distance of more than six miles before he brought up at the point from which he had started. The mountain was completely surrounded by boiling, fuming sulphurous water!

Disheartened by his discovery, and at the point of exhaustion, Grandon sat down on a boulder to plan his next move. Obviously he could not hope to rescue the girl now. No doubt she was already dead, or would be soon.

No, he could not save her, but he would die avenging her.

As he rose to carry out his purpose, his attention was attracted by an airship, similar in shape to Vorn Vangal's, but considerably larger, flying low over the rocky hills. While he watched, it made a landing less than a quarter of a mile from him, and two men stepped from the cab. Without a moment's hesitation, Grandon ran toward them.

One of the men raised a cylindrical object to his eyes, evidently a telescope, and pointed it toward the mountain. He gazed for some time, then handed it to his companion. Both were so engrossed by the strange sight before them they did not see two menacing forms swooping down on them from behind.

Grandon saw, and shouted a warning, but too late. The curved talons hooked their quarry with unerring precision, and both men were carried struggling, out over the boiling water.

The man with the telescope turned and beat his assailant with the instrument, gripping the furry belly with one hand as he swung the weapon with the other. Apparently he succeeded in breaking a wing, for the captor and captive plunged to death a moment later. The other Olban, still struggling, was carried out of sight.

Saddened and infuriated, Grandon walked to the airship. Just as he reached the side of the craft, darkness descended.

Grandon groped his way to the Olban airship in the pitchy darkness. While it was yet light, he had noticed the side door of the dome-like cab stood open. A brilliant flash from the volcano, reflected by the clouds, the boiling water, and the crystal dome, showed him his objective. He entered the cab and closed the door.

Moving his hands carefully about the interior, he felt two cushioned seats and a number of handles, levers and buttons. At random, he pressed a small button, whereupon a tiny light cast its radiance down on him from the top of the dome.

For a moment he was bewildered by the imposing array of levers, handles and buttons. Then, to his delight, he saw that each was marked in the simple phonetic characters of the universal language which had been taught him by Vorn Vangal.

He seized a lever marked "Cab Control" and moved it to the left. Immediately the cab revolved to the right, sliding smoothly and noiselessly. He pressed downward on the lever and the cab slanted backward. Being in the form of a perfect sphere it could not only be turned from side to side, but could be tilted forward and backward in its socket. Upon his straightening the lever, the cab resumed its original position.

The advantage of such an arrangement was obvious. From the front of the craft, to right and left, projected two guns labeled "Mattork." The mattorks were weapons similar in construction to torks, but much larger, and firing projectiles of far heavier caliber. Another projected through the keel. By a touch of the cab control lever these mattorks could be trained on an enemy in any position.

Grandon loaded one mattork with explosive metal bullets and the other with deadly glass bullets; the keel-mattork was already loaded with explosive metal bullets. What a battle he would give the accursed grampites in the morning!

Constant thoughts of Vernia dominated his mind. His reason told him that she was dead, but despite this, hope persisted.

As he hoped, he wished intensely — earnestly. Then suddenly his wish bore fruit, for the airship began slowly to rise from the ground.

He had once listened, with scant attention, to a lecture by a noted para-psychologist. He recalled dimly the assertion that every living human being is endowed at birth with all the power of telekinesis after a fashion, but needed practice to develop and perfect it. Before making for the mountain he sailed about in the air for a considerable time, practicing the turning, elevating, and lowering of his craft by purely mental control. At length, feeling that he was master of the airship, he made for the mountain peak.

Very cautiously he made a landing on the outer rim of the crater, then crept to the top to reconnoiter. As he peered over the brink, it was as if the most terrible dreams of Milton and Dante had been fused into one to form the fearful reality before him. There in the blood-red glow of the molten lava swarmed thousands of the demoniac inhabitants of this planetary inferno, croaking hoarsely to each other as they moved about on the ledges or fluttered from place to place. Mingled in the bedlam of sounds that came up to him, were the bleating and cries of countless animals in the pits.

Directly beneath him, a huge grampite emerged from a cave and heaved a human body far out into the fiery lake. Grandon recognized the uniform of the Olban officer who had been captured at the side of the airship, a few hours before.

Grandon walked stealthily around the edge of the pit, hoping to find some path by which he might make his way, unnoticed, to the ledges beneath. He had gone perhaps a third of the way around the mountain top when he heard a scream of terror. It was the voice of Vernia.

Startled to instant action, Grandon scrambled and slid precipitately down to the top ledge, leaped the ten feet to the second and a like distance to the third, and ran directly to the pit from which the sounds emanated. Twelve feet down he saw Vernia struggling with her captor, while two terrified little animals hugged the wall. In an instant he was at her side. A stroke of his blade severed the arm that gripped her; another sent the head of the monster rolling.

"Come," he said, "we must get out of here at once."

"But how?" she asked. "The walls are as smooth as glass. I'm afraid escape from this pit is impossible. If we could fly . . ."

Her words were cut short by an onslaught from above. Grandon had been seen and a general alarm had been sounded.

With his back to the wall and the girl crouching at his side, Grandon fought desperately with sword and knife. The pile of carcasses before him grew breast high before he realized that they were likely to be smothered beneath them. Calling to the girl to follow, he leaped atop the pile, and fought from that position. After that he constantly shifted from side to side, while the pit continued to fill with slain assailants, who came on in increasing numbers.

Torn and bleeding from many wounds, he at length stood with head and shoulders above the edge of the pit. This left him open to attack from the rear, and forced him to adopt new tactics. Bringing his tork into play, he sent a spray of bullets about him in a circle, temporarily demoralizing the attackers. The slight respite gave him time to assist Vernia from the pit, and together they ran into the cave.

They found a narrow passageway at the back of the cave, and groped their way in the blackness for some distance before they came to another narrow gallery crossing it at right angles. Soon they were in a veritable labyrinth of caves and galleries, leading farther into the mountain.

They had wandered for more than an hour in the subterranean maze when a narrow-lighted opening appeared ahead. Very cautiously Grandon led the way toward this opening, hoping it would offer an avenue of escape. When they were within a short distance of it, he went ahead alone to reconnoiter. A moment later he returned, enjoining the utmost silence to his companion, and together they tiptoed forward.

They were at the rear door of a cave similar to the one through which they had entered the mountain, but considerably larger. Within was a grampite family in repose. There were twelve individuals in the family group, the huge male, his mate, six tiny specimens on which the down had just begun to appear, and four about half grown, all hanging upside down by their sharp, curved toenails, which were hooked in crevices in the wall. The father of the family hung near the cave mouth, the mother depended from one side with the six members of her latest litter beside her, and the half grown offsprings occupied positions on the opposite wall.

"Come," he whispered. "I believe we can get out without disturbing them. If they waken I will use the tork."

Very quietly, they made their way toward the cave mouth. When they reached the center of the floor the male grampite stirred uneasily, and Grandon held the weapon in readiness, but the creature merely stretched one wing a bit, then folded it and resumed his slumber. A moment later they stood on the topmost ledge with fifteen feet of steep crater wall to negotiate before they could reach the rim.

They succeeded in clambering to the top, unobserved, and to his inestimable relief, Grandon sighted the glistening dome of the Olban airship only a hundred yards from where they emerged.

Vernia's eyes were wide with amazement as he opened the door of the cab and seated her on the cushions. "An Olban airship!" she gasped. "Where did you get it? Why, I thought only trained Olban officers could run them."

While she spoke, they were mounting high in the air. She turned and looked him squarely in the eyes. "Grandon of Terra, have you deceived me? Are you of Olba?"

He related how he had acquired the airship, and she shuddered as he told of the death of the two officers who had brought it thither.

"As for deceiving you, my princess," he concluded, "I should sooner tear out my right eye."

She laid her hand gently on his arm. "It makes me very happy to hear you say that."

He thrilled at her touch and words, but did not turn his head. The craft was now poised far above the glowing crater.

"What are you going to do?" she asked.

"I'm going to teach those devils a lesson," he replied. "The ship of the two men they murdered will now wreak vengeance on them."

They descended swiftly until the airship was on a level with the topmost ledge. Grandon pulled the cab control lever, until both mattorks were trained over the side, then circled the crater and poured a deadly fusillade among the bewildered grampites. Soon the air was black with the creatures, dozens of whom attacked the craft, but without success. A number of them swarmed on the deck and endeavored to get at the inmates of the cab.

"Give me your tork," said Vernia.

He unbuckled his belt and handed her the weapon. She opened the door a little way and soon cleared the deck of enemies. Then, while Grandon raked ledge after ledge, she shot down those of the flying attackers who came within range. Most of them fell into the fiery lake, and soon the air was filled with the stench of scorched flesh and hair.

For more than an hour they circled the crater, at the end of which time not a living grampite was in sight. The ledges were strewn with carcasses, and the lake of lava was sending up black clouds of smoke as it consumed those brought down by the tork. Grandon estimated that at least two-thirds of the population of that crater had been exterminated; the others had been driven to cover.

The avenging craft again rose high above the mountain.

"Now to return you to Reabon," said Grandon. "Can you tell me which way it lies from here?"

"As I recall it, this place lies across the Azpok Ocean, directly south of Reabon. If you will steer due north, we should be able to arrive on ground that will be familiar to me, and we can then easily make our way to the capital."

Grandon examined the Olban compass, which hung suspended by a tiny wire in the front of the cab. "I presume that, as in my own world, the compass always points toward the north."

"It should," replied Vernia, "unless deflected by some counter magnetic attraction."

Grandon set his course accordingly, traveling swiftly at a height of approximately two thousand feet.

The ship was amply stored with provisions and water, and they ate their first food in nearly twenty-four hours while hurtling through space at a terrific rate of speed.

"Try to go to sleep now," said Grandon. "In a few hours you will be safely home, and I will return to my faithful mountaineers. Then we can continue our war."

"What if I should not choose to move against Uxpo?"

"You would save the useless waste of thousands of human lives, and therefore place me eternally in your debt."

"You have already put me under an obligation to you for which my entire empire would not be sufficient recompense. Since you will not accept the second highest office in Zarovia, I have decided to free Uxpo. We shall be neighbors and, I hope, friends."

"In the name of the people of Uxpo, I thank you for your generous decision, and . . ."

He was interrupted by a series of rude shocks and a rending crash as they came to a complete standstill. Both were thrown violently against the front of the cab. Grandon struck his head on the butt of a mattork and lost consciousness. Vernia was more fortunate, as she fell feet foremost, although her ankle received a bad wrench.

When she saw Grandon's face, pale as death, and the blood flowing from an ugly cut on his forehead, she flung herself down beside him and took his head on her lap. To her relief, she heard the beating of his heart when she placed her ear to his breast. Opening one of the provision drawers, she extracted a flask of water and bathed his face.

Presently he opened his eyes.

"What happened?" he asked. "What struck us?"

"I do not know," she replied. "Lie quietly while I dress your wound. Then we will investigate."

CHAPTER IX

Grandon protested that the jagged wound in his forehead was a mere scratch, but Vernia insisted on binding it for him, and did so with adroitness.

When she finished, he rose dizzily and opened the door of the cab. A pungent odor assailed their nostrils, an odor similar to that produced by pouring sulfuric acid on copper.

He switched on the forward searchlight, which revealed the shattered front of their craft jammed against an enormous tree-trunk. The keel rested in a forked branch, which kept them from falling. A thin column of vapor curled upward from the shattered hull, emitting the stifling odor that had greeted them when they opened the door.

"I guess we are done with flying," said Grandon, eyeing the wreck askance. "At least, we will fly no more with this airship."

"Is it so badly broken?"

"The power mechanism is destroyed. An Olban once told me that a phial of acid was placed within each mechanism in such a fashion that it would instantly destroy it if tampered with. Evidently the shock of our encounter with the tree trunk broke the phial, for the fumes are unmistakably those of acid on metal."

Grandon flashed the searchlight above them in an effort to ascertain where they were, but above, below and around them on every side they could see only branches and leaves. And such leaves! They were spatulate in shape, and a dark glossy green in color, varying between fifteen and twenty feet in length, while the stems were from eight to twelve inches thick. Each twig would have made a good-sized fern tree, while the trunk against which their craft had jammed was a full fifty feet in thickness.

"Not much use to do any exploring before morning, I guess," said Grandon. "This is a giant of a tree. In what part of Reabon do these trees grow, and what do you call them?"

"There are no trees like this in Reabon," replied Vernia, "nor was I aware that there were such trees anywhere on Zarovia. Are you positive that we have been traveling due north?"

Grandon glanced at the compass. "Strange," he said. "Just a moment before we struck, the needle pointed in a direction in which we were traveling. Now it points at right angles to the keel. Something must have been broken by the grampites. I'm afraid we'll have to wait until the sun rises to get our bearings."

"We can at least be positive of two things. That we are not in

Reabon, and that we are in some unexplored part of Zarovia."

At dawn, Grandon made his way down the tree trunk, clinging to the rough, curling bark with fingers and toes. It was a long, perilous descent, a matter of at least a thousand feet, and he guessed half an hour must have elapsed before he stood on the ground.

The forest giant under which he stood was more than a hundred feet in diameter at the base. All about him, as far as he could see, were many more like it. He noticed that all of the trees were connected by broad surface roots, and this fact, together with the total absence of spores or seeds, apprised him of the reason why these trees were, in all probability, confined to a single locality.

They must have begun and evolved on this part of the planet without developing other means of propagation than that of sending out surface roots to form new plants at some distance from the parent trees. Consequently their spread would be regulated, not only by the number of new trees they could produce in this manner, but by the character of the surrounding country as well, for any barrier such as a body of water or a stretch of barren, rocky land would effectually check their progress.

Marking his trail by slashing trees or surface roots with his knife as he passed along, Grandon started his journey of exploration. He felt like a pygmy, as he walked beneath those mighty spires of wood, treading matted, molding leaves that were nearly as long as the airship, and climbing over surface roots so thick that often he could not see over them. After he had traveled thus for more than half an hour he saw a number of tall, conical mounds ahead of him, and judged from the regularity of their construction, that they housed human beings. As he approached more closely he observed that they were all dotted here and there with round holes about four feet in diameter.

He arrived within fifty feet of the nearest mound without noting any signs of animal life, and, concluding that it must be deserted, stepped boldly forward. Then, without the slightest hint of warning, something darted out suddenly and ran toward him on its six horny legs with incredible swiftness.

The creature was about the size of a small Shetland pony, with eyes as big as dinner plates set in a head more than two feet across and surmounted by two long, jointed antennae, its jaws armed with sharp mandibles and a pair of forceps large enough to encircle two men. The entire body was covered with glistening ivory-white armor. It came at him with forceps outspread.

In a moment, Grandon found that his tork had no effect; a moment later, he found his sword equally useless. The forceps encircled him, and he was dragged into the dark hole.

Vernia stepped out of the airship and climbed the projecting bark of the tree; it had been over two hours since Grandon left, and she was worried. From a height of several hundred feet above the airship, she peered through the thick curtain of leaves and saw that this tree stood in a narrow valley. The encircling mountains were bare, but the valley itself was filled with giant trees.

She looked down to see a white, six-legged monster scuttling up the trunk, carrying a smaller, bright green creature in its forceps. It turned out on a limb just below her, to deposit its burden on one of the large leaves.

The green thing had six legs, but its plump body was oval-shaped, with the head set at the narrow end and two sharp horns protruding just above the posterior extremity. As soon as it was put down, it uncoiled a long, slender sucking tube which it inserted in the leaf.

Vernia was both mystified and frightened. She flattened out on the limb, and peered cautiously over the edge.

To her infinite terror she saw many more mounting the tree and depositing their burdens here and there until it literally swarmed with the white things and their green charges. Glancing across to the next tree, she saw that it was similarly infested, and shuddered at the thought that the monsters might soon climb to where she was concealed.

Then, she saw a number of naked, hairy men ascending the tree. Each man carried a sack slung over his shoulder and fastened in place by a strap. She noticed that there appeared to be no animosity between the men and the monsters, and concluded that the great ant-like creatures must have been domesticated by these cavemen.

Her supposition was strengthened by the sight of one of the men obtaining a white, sticky substance from one of the green things, with the aid of a white one, which titillated the posterior horns of its smaller green charge, causing it to exude the material into the sack which the man carried. All the other men were engaged in the same task, going from leaf to leaf until their sacks were filled, then carrying them down the tree.

A man who moved more slowly than his fellows was nipped sharply by one of the white creatures. He gave a cry of pain and hurried his step. Then it dawned on her that the men were the slaves and the monsters their masters.

She was reflecting on this paradox when one of the white

things, which had mounted on the opposite side of the tree unobserved by her, took a notion to carry its green charge out on the limb she occupied. She rose hurriedly and ran toward the swaying tip, but the creature deposited its burden on the leaf and darted after her with amazing speed. She had only gone a few steps when the powerful forceps encircled her.

Her captor appeared able to travel on the rough tree trunk upside down or right side up with equal facility, and carried her down to the ground at a terrific rate of speed. When it reached the ground it made off under the giant tree, climbing over the thick surface roots with great ease, and at length brought up at the entrance of a conical dwelling about a hundred feet in height.

It paused there for a moment, touched its antennae to those of a similar creature which appeared to be guarding the doorway, then carried her through a maze of dark runways to a dimly-lighted underground chamber. It laid her on the floor at the feet of an individual, apparently of the same species. This new monster had a white body and similar brown forceps and mandibles, and, in addition, a large pair of transparent wings. Its abdomen was distended to more than ten times the size of that of her captor.

Vernia rose to her feet and faced the thing before her, expecting to be seized and devoured. It looked at her searchingly for a moment, then vibrated its antennae noiselessly. Another white creature, similar to her captor in shape, but smaller, and lacking the huge forceps, appeared as if in answer to a summons.

Each vibrated its antennae in turn, then the newcomer pushed Vernia toward one of the runways. She could not mistake the meaning of this movement. Stooping to avoid the low ceiling, she entered and walked forward in the darkness. When she had traveled a short distance her conductor pushed her into a cross-runway that ended in a large, round chamber with a dome-like roof.

This room was lighted by a great central opening, and contained more than a hundred girls and women, who were busily engaged in separating round white balls about an inch in diameter, which cohered in glutinous masses, and placing them in small holes that honeycombed the walls on all sides.

Her guide turned her over to a woman who seemed to be a sort of superintendent or overseer, and departed.

The woman looked at her curiously and, to her surprise, addressed her in patoa. "Who are you, girl, and how came you here!"

"I am Vernia of Reabon, and was just now captured by one of those fierce white creatures with the huge forceps."

"You were captured by a soldier sabit, but it is evident that you are from some distant part of the world, for here people do not go about wrapped in brightly colored skins, such as you wear."

Judging from those representatives of the human race which she had seen so far in the valley, Vernia could well believe this statement, for neither the men she had seen in the tree nor the women who now surrounded her were clothed. The women, like the men, were quite hairy; they were also big-boned, low-browed and coarse-featured.

"I presume my country *is* far from here," Vernia said, "for I have never heard either of trees or creatures such as you have in this locality, although I know all that is known by our people about Zarovian geography. I have not the slightest idea where I am."

"You are in the Valley of the Sabits, which is in the center of the great salt marshes where my people live. When but a young girl I was captured by a slaving party and brought hither, even as you were captured and brought just now, to spend the rest of your life serving the masters of men. Enough of this talk for the present. There are no idlers here, and you must work with the others. Here, Rotha," calling a young girl who toiled nearby, "a new slave who calls herself Vernia of Reabon. Acquaint her with the nature of our work."

The girl flashed a friendly smile at Vernia, and showed her how to separate the white balls, which she explained were sabit eggs, and stow them in their cells. She was much better-looking than those around her, appearing more like the women of the civilized races.

Vernia shuddered at the feel of the sticky, plasmic mass of eggs that was handed her, but nevertheless went to work with a will, and soon became nearly as adept as those about her.

Rotha was communicative, and talked incessantly as she worked. She had been born in captivity, so knew of the ways of her ancestors, the marsh people, only through the lips of others. She was, however, the granddaughter of a soldier of Mernerum who had married a marsh woman, which accounted for her superior intelligence and beauty.

The sabits, she said, were divided into many communities, and the inhabitants of any given community might be recognized by their markings. Those of their own community were known by their brown forceps and mandibles, there were others with black forceps and mandibles, others with green, red, *et cetera*. The largest and greatest community of all was that of the sabits who were pure white.

In each community there were four kinds of individuals. The

greatest and most powerful was the single queen sabit, or female ruler, who had ordered Vernia sent hither. She was winged, and, when fertile, swelled to many times the size of the others.

Next to her in importance was the king sabit, her mate. He was the only male permitted to live in the community, and was winged like the queen, but much smaller. The other two kinds were known as workers and soldiers. The former were comparatively diminutive in size and inefficient in battle, while the soldier sabits were large, powerful, and armed with huge forceps. Both workers and soldiers were wingless and sexless.

The queen sabit did little else than eat, sleep and lay thousands of these white, sticky eggs. Her mate was active in administering the affairs of the community, subject always to her approval and consent.

"But why is it," asked Vernia, "that these men submit to the domination of creatures of a lower order? Why, my soldiers kill and drive off creatures a thousand times more terrible than these."

"They may be more terrible physically," said Rotha, "but mentally the sabits are superior to all other beasts. True, they all think in the same way, along the same lines, and all the sabits will react to any situation in the same way, but this only makes them the more formidable, for they thus act in perfect unison in cases of emergencies. A sabit community may be likened to a single animal, with the queen as the head, directing all operations, the king as the eyes looking here and there and everywhere to see that the directions are properly carried out, and the soldiers and workers, as the arms and legs, supplying every want of the body and protecting it from all dangers."

"But even so, may not men, with torks, scarbos, spears and knives, slay them as easily as they do the great beasts?"

"I know nothing of the weapons you call torks, nor have I ever heard that the marsh people use them. Spears, scarbos, knives and clubs they have, but these avail them little against the armored sabits. I have heard that a very powerful man may subdue a sabit by striking him between the eyes with a heavy club, but this is a most difficult feat, as they move with exceeding swiftness, and blows on any other spot are to no effect. It is said that these creatures have three brains, one in the head, one in the thorax and one in the abdomen, so that even if one is destroyed the other two may function for days afterward."

"Then, in order to kill one sabit a warrior must virtually kill three! But tell me now of yourself, and of the marsh people."

"About myself . . ." Rotha began, then checked her speech to stare at an approaching procession of worker sabits. "It is time for eating."

The sabits carried pouches from which they distributed a sticky mixture composed of a white, mucilaginous substance in which small edible fungi had been stirred. The girls and women instantly ceased work at their approach, and eagerly devoured their portions of proffered food. Although Vernia was exceedingly hungry, she could not bring herself to touch the sticky mess, but divided it among those about her.

When they had finished, Rotha said: "I must leave you now, Vernia of Reabon, for tonight is my mating night, and there comes the soldier who will take me away. Tomorrow night I will be with you, and from then on for some time, but for a full day and night I will be absent."

"What mean you by the mating night, and why, if you are to be mated, will you be absent for but one night?"

Rotha sighed. "It is the custom here," she replied. "In this valley men and women who are mated do not live together as in the outer world, nor have they even the privilege of choosing their own mates."

"You mean that they are mated against their wishes?"

"In this valley is it useless to wish. There is no law but the will of the masters, and it is their purpose to produce a stronger and more beautiful race of slaves. Having just come of age, I have been selected to do my part."

"But you know naught of love here? Do you willingly submit to the treatment usually accorded domestic animals?"

"Speak not of love, Vernia of Reabon, for Oro the Mighty is large and strong and beautiful — oh, so beautiful, my Vernia — and excels the others in all things. But I know it will not — it cannot be Oro, as the king sabit will not choose him for the mating pens. A slight blemish, a birthmark on his left shoulder, disqualifies him. Because of his great strength, however, he had been chosen chief keeper, or guard, of the pens, to maintain peace among the others and see that things are conducted in an orderly fashion. Oro, my beloved, will perhaps be the one to receive me at the gate, the one to take me to that awful room; but even he, with all his mighty strength, will be unable to save me . . ."

CHAPTER X

Grandon fought unavailingly with his sword as he was dragged into the dark burrow. He found a crevice in the armor of his captor, whereupon it stopped and shook him until his head reeled and the weapon dropped from his hand. Then the sabit carried him to the great central room, in which were the king and queen sabits of the white community.

As soon as he was dropped to the floor, the king sabit leaped on him and, cutting his belt with sharp mandibles, removed his tork and knife. Grandon sat up weakly.

After looking at him fixedly for some time the queen sabit summoned two workers by vibrating her antennae, and he was conducted through a series of runways and tunnels to a great, light chamber, where hundreds of naked, hairy men were engaged in the task of receiving sacks filled with a sticky white mixture from men who brought them to the doorway. They then fed the contents to thousands of fat, white, grub-like creatures that varied in size from two to eight feet in length. He saw one of the larger grubs near him bite a mouthful of flesh from the shoulder of its tender; a little farther away two men held a huge grub while a third endeavored to reach its swaying head with a sackful of sticky food.

His conductors piloted him among the swaying, wriggling grubs and scurrying men to where a single individual taller than his fellows stood with folded arms, apparently supervising the work. One of the sabits vibrated its antennae, this time creating a series of musical tones. The man turned, replied with three musical tones, and took Grandon by the arm, whereupon the two sabits left him.

"A new slave, eh?" he said gruffly. "Don't stand there staring like a stupid ptang. You have eyes to see the nature of the task before you. Begin it quickly, before you have painful cause to regret your slowness."

Grandon coolly surveyed the great brute before him. His low forehead was crossed by a livid scar just above the beetling brows, from beneath which his small, beady eyes glared. His right ear had been completely torn away, and with it a portion of the surrounding scalp.

"I have eyes to see and ears to hear that which pleases me not," Grandon replied. "You accuse me of the stupidity of a ptang, but I must needs have the stupidity of a thousand ptangs to obey this thing miscalled a man which stands before me."

The overseer's thick lips drew back; with lightning-like quickness he directed a blow at Grandon's head. By ducking swiftly the Earthman avoided the full force of the blow which, glancing though it was, sent him reeling to the floor a full twenty feet away.

"You would insult Od, would you?" the overseer snarled. "You would refuse to feed the fantas. Miserable, misbegotten offspring of misguided parents, then shall your torn body feed them, and that speedily."

He sprang and lifted his heavy foot for a kick; Grandon executed a quick scissors movement with his legs, and his assailant fell sprawling.

Both men leaped to their feet in an instant. As they faced each other, the slaves abandoned their wriggling fanta charges and formed an excited ring about the pair. The giant Od was first annoyed, then amazed, at his inability to strike his opponent, while blows rained incessantly against his unguarded chin and solar plexus. At length, he abandoned all thought of striking his elusive antagonist and leaped forward to clutch him.

It was the opening for which Grandon had been waiting. Stepping lightly to one side, he planted a terrific blow behind the ragged ear. Od reeled blindly for a moment, then fell prone, where he lay limp and still. A shout of approval went up from the group of spectators; then a cry from a man near the door checked their cheering. "To your tasks, quickly! The sabits are coming!"

They scattered, and when four soldier sabits arrived all but Grandon and Od were busily tending their fractious charges. The sabits spied Grandon, standing with heaving breast beside his prostrate foe, and ran quickly to where he stood. One of them looked inquiringly at him, and vibrated its antennae, producing a series of tones. When it received no reply it brought a slave from nearby and repeated the vibrations. The slave replied, using his voice to produce various tones, and Grandon judged from his gestures that he was describing the combat.

Immediately one of the sabits made for the door, and shortly returned with the winged king. Then there was a further vibratory conversation, this time among the sabits. Grandon noticed that when they communicated with each other the vibrations were noiseless.

Momentarily expecting to be punished, Grandon was amazed when the four soldier sabits suddenly leaped to the prostrate man and tore him to pieces. These pieces were distributed among the nearby grubs.

Then the king sabit again vibrated his antennae, this time producing musical tones, and the slave translated for Grandon. "By order of the king sabit you are to assume immediately the duties of the man you just defeated; by vanquishing Od, greatest of all of us in the community, you have demonstrated your eligibility for the office."

"But I know nothing of these duties," remonstrated Grandon.

"It does not matter. The men know what is to be done. You are simply to maintain order and see that there is no idling. A soldier sabit will remain with you for a few days to teach you the tone language so that thereafter you may receive your orders direct from the sabits."

The working day of the sabits and their slaves began at dawn and continued until darkness. The slaves were fed twice daily, once upon rising and once when the day's work was completed. The diet was always the same — a mixture of the sweet, sticky stuff and edible fungi.

With the coming of darkness all members of the community were herded within the conical clay house and the burrows which connected them. A sleeping room with bare dirt floors was set aside for the men and carefully guarded by soldier sabits. A separate dormitory for the women and children was similarly guarded. Men and women were not allowed to mingle during the day, and though they might see each other from a distance seldom had opportunities even for conversation.

Grandon watched carefully for an opportunity to escape and return to Vernia, but it seemed that his every movement was anticipated by the watchful sabits. He learned the tone language readily, and after several weeks had elapsed, became fairly familiar with his surroundings and the mode of life of the strange creatures who had captured him. His instructor told him how the fantas were hatched from the eggs laid by the roga. They were tended and fed by women and girls until they reached a size that made it necessary for the men to take charge of them. When they had grown larger than adults, they were taken to a dark room deep under the ground, where they spun great, tough cocoons that completely surrounded them, and lay dormant in these, finally emerging as full-fledged adult sabits.

Many days passed before Grandon was even permitted out of doors. Then, one morning, he was placed in charge of a crew of food carriers, and the white soldier sabits, taking their "cattle," the green creatures, to their leafy pastures, led the way directly to the tree in which the airship was dammed.

Grandon had mounted to gather the sweet torlage. After a tedious climb he saw the craft directly above him. Slaves, sabits and the green "cattle" swarmed all about it without paying it the slightest attention.

Grandon moved cautiously toward the forked limb on which it rested, and peered within the cab. It was empty, and apparently open; he selected a knife and a small flashlight from the miscellaneous articles it contained, secreting them beneath his clothing.

As there were no signs of a struggle he assumed that Vernia had left voluntarily; but he was equally certain that she could not have gone far without being captured and enslaved by the sabits.

Having by this time become familiar with the fate of female slaves of marriageable age, Grandon resolved that she must be rescued speedily. There were hundreds of sabit communities in the valley, in any one of which she might be a prisoner; he must find a way to escape from his own community, then spy on all the others in turn until he found her.

That night when the men had been quartered in their dormitory he thought of a plan, and set about at once to put it into execution.

On the evening following her capture, Vernia was choking down a small portion of the sticky mess when she saw Rotha entering the women's quarters.

The girl ran toward her and buried her face in her bosom, weeping softly. Vernia noticed several bruises on her shoulders and arms, and the bluish prints of huge fingers on her neck.

"Poor child," Vernia murmured. "They have abused you shamefully."

The girl looked up into her eyes, and there was a smile on her quivering lips. "I weep not with sorrow, Vernia of Reabon," she whispered. "It is because of my great joy that I cannot control myself. I tremble with rapture and thrill with the memory of a wonderful experience."

"But you have been choked and beaten."

"You do not understand. The man who made those marks is dead."

"Then you were rescued. Tell me of it."

"When I entered the mating pens, Oro, whom I love, met me at the gate and conducted me to the man for whom I had been destined by the king sabit. On the way I besought him to take me to an empty room and leave me there until tonight, but he said such tactics would be useless — that we would surely be found out and the sabits would put us both to death with horrible tortures.

"When he led me into the room, a great, hairy man leaped up from the corner and seized me by the arms. I cried out and struggled to escape him. Oro had left, but he must have heard me cry, for I saw him enter the room just as the hairy giant hurled me to the floor.

"Would that you could have seen my beloved at the moment, my Vernia! He was magnificent. With blazing eyes and set lips he grasped my assailant, held him for a moment aloft, and then threw him to the floor with such violence that I could hear the snapping of his bones. He stood glowering down at the lifeless form for a moment, then lifted me tenderly in his arms, and whispered words of comfort, cuddling me as one would a little child. Presently he set me on my feet and would have gone away, but I begged him not to leave me.

"'Tempt me not,' he said, 'lest I further transgress the laws of our masters, the sabits. Think you that I am fashioned of stone?'

"Then he swept me in his arms, and pressed his lips to mine, while I trembled and grew weak with the joy of that first kiss of love. And so it came about that Oro the Mighty made me his mate, and swore that I was his, and he was mine, forever and ever. Is it not wonderful?"

"It is wonderful," said Vernia, "to have known your true love, though for only a day. But will Oro not be punished by the sabits?"

"If he is found out. But during the night he took the body to the river and, after weighting it with stones, sank it in deep water. The natural supposition will be that he man escaped."

Vernia and Rotha worked side by side for many days, first in the incubator room, and later tending and feeding small fantas. It was due to this change in occupation that Vernia twice avoided the inspection tours of the king sabit.

She was feeding sticky stuff to a voracious young fanta one day when Rotha touched her arm. "The king sabit comes. Stoop over that he may not observe you."

Vernia bent low over the wriggling fanta, meanwhile watching the king sabit from the corner of her eye. He advanced slowly, pausing now and then to indicate a woman for the pens. At length he came in front of Vernia, stopped for a moment, then started on. It was her hungry charge that proved her undoing, for in her preoccupation, she held her wrist too close to the keen mandibles and received a sharp nip.

With a cry of pain she stood erect. The king sabit stopped, turned back, looked at her fixedly for a moment, then vibrated his antennae. She would be conducted to the mating pens the following evening.

CHAPTER XI

Grandon's plan of escape entailed no inconsiderable degree of caution, as well as an immense amount of physical labor.

The room adjoining the dormitory in which he and his men were quartered was used for storing the driest fungi which, when mixed with the sticky milk of the green creatures, constituted the food of the slaves. These fungi were dumped in great heaps about the room without any semblance of order, and as one of the heaps effectually concealed a corner, one side of which was formed by the outer wall, it was Grandon's purpose to dig a tunnel from this point to a spot he had marked about fifty feet from the hut, where he could emerge under a large surface root. The entrance to his tunnel would thus be hidden by the pile of fungi, while the exit might easily be covered with one of the huge leaves, a profusion of which lay everywhere about the hut.

Night after night he labored, digging with bare hands and the knife he had brought from the airship, for he had no tools of any kind. After many nights of arduous toil he had completed a slanting tunnel about eight feet deep, and was digging in a horizontal direction toward the point where he had calculated the root would be, when the floor of his burrow gave way with startling abruptness. He fell, first striking some objects that gave off a metallic clang, then alighting on a hard, smooth surface with considerable force.

Dazed for a moment, Grandon lay there in pitch darkness with no inkling of what had happened. At length he arose stiffly to his feet, for he was badly bruised, though fortunately no bones were broken. He bethought himself now of the flashlight which he had kept concealed in his clothing since the day he had examined the abandoned airship.

The beating of his heart was momentarily stilled by the sight which greeted his eyes when he turned on the light; directly in front of him stood what appeared to be a huge warrior, attired in armor from head to foot. Closer scrutiny, however, revealed the fact that he faced an empty suit of armor, for a mailed gauntlet clutching a heavy axe had fallen from one of the arms. It was this which had caused the clanging sound he had head.

The armor was skillfully wrought of a brownish metal which he at first took for bronze on account of its appearance. It was of a pattern unlike anything he had ever seen or heard of, and strikingly decorated with designs of inlaid gold set with brilliant jewels.

Sharp metal spines projected from the top and back of the grotesque headpiece, while two large green jewels sparkled just above the movable visor like the eyes of some multi-horned reptile. In the visor itself, the true eyeholes were of a hard, thick crystal, and below them were small perforations to admit air. A huge broadsword hung from one side of the belt and a short club with a heavy spiked knob dangled from the other.

On the floor before the figure lay a quantity of loose earth which had been carried with Grandon in his fall. He dashed the light upward and its rays revealed a ceiling nearly ten feet above his head, supported by timbers. He had broken through between two of the large timbers at a point where the crosspieces were completely rotted away.

Upon examining his surroundings he found that he was in a corridor about thirty feet in width, and extending in both directions as far as he could see. A double row of hexagonal columns supported the heavy ceiling beams, and before each column stood a figure similar to the one he had examined, with the exception that every alternate figure held a long, broad-bladed spear instead of an axe in the extended right gauntlet.

The Earthman was in a quandary; he could not return via the opening through which he had fallen.

From his fellow slaves he had heard legends of an ancient race of men called Albines, who were said to have at one time been masters of the sabits. These Albines wore suits of mail which effectively protected them from the creatures, and made slaves of whole colonies by raiding them and making prisoners of the queen and king sabits, for the soldiers and workers, being ever subject to the commands of their rulers, immediately became docile when the lives of their superiors were threatened. The Albines had vanished many years before — no one knew how or why — and the sabits had thenceforth turned the tables on men by enslaving the marsh-people.

Grandon selected a suit of armor which appeared to be his size, and after a considerable struggle with the unfamiliar fastenings, succeeded in donning it. He had expected to feel stiff and awkward in his metal suit, and was therefore agreeably surprised when he found it both light and pliable; for though exceedingly hard and strong, the metal was as light as aluminum and so fashioned that the interlocking plates easily adjusted themselves to every movement of the body.

Armed with sword, axe and club, he set out to explore the subterranean passageway, walking between the two rows of pillars that were guarded by the silent sentinels of a vanished race, and flashing his light in a semicircle before him.

As he passed along, he noticed that the stone walls on both sides of him were carved at intervals with scenes and hieroglyphics. The scenes, for the most part, represented men attired in armor such as he wore, battling with sabits. He noticed, also, that in nearly every instance, the figures were pictured as striking the sabits between the eyes with spiked clubs, although a few used axes; and one was represented as severing a soldier sabit's head from its body with a broadsword.

One scene that particularly interested him depicted a group of Albines in the act of capturing a queen sabit while their comrades fought off her guards. They were fastening huge manacles on her neck and legs while she struggled desperately.

It seemed that he had walked for more than a mile along the corridor, and passed several thousand armored figures, when he arrived at a great circular chamber that, for elegance and richness of decoration, surpassed anything he had ever seen.

From the base of the walls to the peak of the dome-like ceiling, it was a mass of grotesque bas-reliefs and mural paintings in bright pigments, while gracefully sculptured statues of men and women occupied niches set in intervals of about fifteen feet all about the room. The floor was of varicolored blocks of clearest crystal, fitted together so skillfully that they presented a surface as smooth as that of a mirror, while forming beautiful tessellated patterns of exquisite design.

When he turned his light on the floor it sent forth myriad reflections that lit up the entire room. He was amazed by this phenomenon until he discovered that the base of each block had been cut and silvered so each beam of light was multiplied a thousand-fold.

In the center of the room a fountain babbled, evidently fed by an artesian well, for it could not otherwise have continued in operation for hundreds of years without attention. As he walked toward the fountain he saw a round bulk, which he had at first mistaken for a shadow, suddenly leap back and then scamper for a broad doorway at the left.

The thing had short legs armed with huge claws that rattled on the polished floor, and a barrel-shaped body covered with tiny, fishlike scales. Grandon recognized it as one of the large, burrowing rodents which the omnivorous sabits prized so highly as an article of food.

Several times he had seen them feeding on fungi and grasses in the woods, and the thought came that this creature must needs have access to the outer world to live; consequently there must undoubtedly be a means of egress nearby which he himself could use, for where so thick-bodied a rodent could go, he could easily follow.

He entered the doorway in quick pursuit and found himself in a passageway similar to the one he had just vacated. The circular chamber was evidently a sort of hub from which these passageways radiated as spokes in all directions.

The rodent had disappeared, but its trail was not hard to follow, for it had left thousands of muddy footprints during its many excursions to the fountain. The trail terminated at a gaping black hole in the wall where a portion of the sculptured stone had broken away. Drawing his sword and pointing the light before him, he entered the dark, winding burrow, crawling on knees and elbows. It led upward in a slanting, irregular spiral which he thought would never come to an end.

At length the welcome scent of fresh air came to his nostrils and he emerged from the burrow at the base of a huge tree. He shut off the light. As he paused there in the darkness, Grandon fancied he heard the distant murmur of human voices. He listened intently for a moment, then clambered up on a large surface root. Several hundred yards away he saw two torches flickering before the gateway of a circular wall about ten feet high which surrounded a tall, conical structure.

Leaping down from the root he approached the place cautiously. As he drew nearer the sounds grew more plain, and he could distinguish the voices of men raised in altercation. He also heard the sound of blows, and thought he detected the faint cry of a woman.

The torch-lit gateway was guarded by two powerful soldier sabits with brown forceps, so he circled, keeping well out of sight, and brought up at the base of the wall at a point that was not visible from the gate. He leaped, hooked his fingers over the edge of the wall, and drew himself up on its broad top. Then, flattening his body on its surface, he peered cautiously within.

The space inside the wall was illuminated by four torches, the sharpened butts of which had been driven in the ground. Some twenty-odd slaves, all big strapping fellows, were ranged in an irregular circle about two of their comrades who were engaged in primitive combat.

Beneath one of the torches lay two other hairy men, stone dead — one with his throat torn out and the other with his head twisted and bent back in such a fashion as to indicate a broken neck.

Suddenly the taller of the two combatants leaped forward and locked his arms about the head of the other, bearing him to the ground. Just as they struck the earth, he whirled, twisting the tightly gripped head — there was a sickening snap, and the duel was ended.

The big fellow arose, panting heavily from his exertions, and faced the others. "You have seen the fate of those three fools," he growled. "Are there any others, who would match their strength with Tholto for this slave woman?"

There was no response. Evidently his comrades were convinced of Tholto's prowess.

"Bring me the woman, Oro," continued the victor. "Many precious moments have I wasted in silencing these braggarts."

A great hairy man, larger even than Tholto and superbly muscled, went into a low door at his back, and emerged a moment later dragging Vernia by the wrist. He pushed her toward Tholto, who seized her roughly and drew her to his side.

The slaves were startled by a clanking noise behind them, and upon looking around beheld a man clad from head to foot in brown armor on which many jewels glistened, his terrifying appearance enhanced by the spine-crested helmet in which two emerald eyes sparkled, and by the businesslike weapons that dangled from his belt.

Straight for the startled Tholto he rushed, and there were none to block his path, for though no living marsh-man had ever seen an Albine, they had been described in detail to all through the familiar legends which held them to be a race of supermen.

"Release the girl," said a clear, commanding voice.

Tholto, though startled, was apparently unafraid. "She belongs to me," he replied. "I will not release her, nor lives there a man or demon who can force me to do so."

"Release the girl or take the consequences, slave! I would not harm you, for your actions are only what might be expected of one with your intelligence and training."

For answer Tholto laughed. His mirth was suddenly cut short by the impact of a mailed fist with the point of his jaw. A look of surprise came to his face; his arms dropped, his knees sagged, and he sank limply to the ground.

Vernia reeled, and would have fallen had not Grandon caught her in his arms. He raised his visor, and, looking into the melting depths of twin pools of flame, saw the soul of a woman.

"How I wished that you would come," she whispered, her arms about his neck, her upturned face so close that the fragrance of her breath intoxicated him, "wished without hope."

For answer he bent low over the yielding, tremulous lips, but their moment of rapture was rudely broken into by a shout from one of the slaves. "The sabits! Run for your lives! The sabits come!"

Grandon wheeled and beheld two soldier sabits rushing toward them. The slaves scattered, diving into the various doorways at the base of the cone-like structure. He pushed the girl into one of these and, lowering his visor, tore the heavy spiked club from his belt.

As the first soldier sabit opened its huge forceps to encircle Grandon's waist, he raised the spiked club and crashed it down with all his might between the two enormous eyes.

The creature paused, its head drooped, and it began walking aimlessly in a circle. Not so its mate, however, which leaped forward and swept Grandon from his feet before he could swing the club a second time. It shook him and crunched him with its powerful mandibles, but the armor plate held, and though giddy from the shaking, he was unhurt.

Grandon lost his spiked club, but his sword and axe remained in his belt. He drew the latter and struck at the creature's foreleg. To his surprise the weapon severed it completely. Where an axe of steel would have failed to make an impression, the razor-like edge of this marvelous metal cut cleanly. Though the axe-head, like the club, was weighted with a ball of black metal, probably lead, the blade itself as well as the handle were of the wondrously hard brown metal.

Encouraged by his success with the axe, Grandon hacked desperately at the ugly head. At length the powerful forceps released their grip and the sabit followed the staggering tactics of its companion, walking about on its five good legs and moving the stump of the sixth as though the member were still there.

The Earthman rose to his feet and struck off the heads of the two creatures with his axe. To his surprise and horror the bodies continued their purposeless wandering!

Vernia came forth from the hut as he was recovering his club, and one by one the marsh-men appeared, astonishment and awe written on their faces. They seemed ready to fall down and worship the hero who had, single-handed, overcome two ferocious soldier sabits.

Tholto, who had laid like a log where Grandon felled him, now sat up and gazed on the proceedings in blank amazement, tenderly feeling his injured jaw, as if fearful that it would come off completely.

"Slaves," said Grandon suddenly, taking the hand of Vernia, "you have offered unspeakable insult to the greatest, the noblest and the most beautiful princess in all Zarovia. Ask her pardon now, for your lives are in her hands."

To a man they groveled before her.

Vernia looked up into the flashing eyes of her champion.

"I would pardon them all, Robert Grandon," she said, "for they know nothing of the ethics of men, but have rather been bred and trained like domestic animals."

"You have heard her generous verdict, slaves," said Grandon. "Rise, now, and attend what I have to say to you. I take it that you would prefer freedom to slavery."

"We desire freedom above all things, mighty Albine," replied Oro, who had taken a place at the head of the men, "but the sabits are all-powerful and may not be overcome by ordinary mortals."

"I am no Albine," continued the Earthman. "Call me Grandon of Terra. What I have done to yonder sabits, you can do to others of their kind. All you need is weapons and armor. These I will provide if you will follow me and acknowledge my leadership."

"I am called Oro the Mighty," the huge marsh-man answered, "yet I gladly acknowledge your leadership."

"And I! And I!" echoed the others with enthusiasm.

"Then follow me and I will make sabit killers of you all."

Grandon led the way toward the gate when he heard a cry behind them. Turning, he beheld Tholto striving weakly to rise.

"Mercy," he cried. "Have mercy, noble Grandon of Terra. Leave me not here to be torn to pieces by sabits and fed to the fantas."

Grandon turned inquiring eyes to Vernia.

"He is the most grievous offender of them all," she said, "yet will I pardon him because of his ignorance."

Motioning two of the men to assist Tholto, Grandon ordered the others to bring as many torches as they could find, but carried only one lighted, and hooded it with a food sack in order that it might not be seen by the sabits.

When all was ready he led them to the mouth of the rodent burrow, enjoining absolute silence on the way. He was the first to enter, with flashlight and sword in his hands as before. Vernia came next, clutching his ankle, and after her came Oro and the others. When they had concluded the tortuous descent and all were standing in the long corridor he ordered that three more torches be lighted and immediately set about the work of outfitting his men with armor and weapons.

No suit of Albine armor small enough for Vernia could be found, but the smallest one available was made to serve the purpose by telescoping it at the waist and fastening it with strips torn from the sack. These sacks were made from the exceedingly tough cocoons spun and eventually discarded by the fantas, and were not only strong and durable, but water-proof as well.

The little army, marching on into the great central room, torch-light glinting from jeweled plates and spears and axes held aloft, looked like reincarnated Albine warriors returned to their ancient haunts.

Grandon assembled his small command near the bubbling fountain and addressed them; "I brought you here with the agreement that I'd free you from the sabits. I had a further plan — to start a movement to free every human slave and make slaves of the sabits that survive! First we will conquer the white sabits, for they are the most powerful. We can attack them from within their own stronghold. On the wall here is a picture of the way the Albines captured sabit rulers, and enslaved their followers. Five men search the passageways and chambers for fetters and chains like those illustrated. Five men will remain here under the command of the princess. The rest will go with me. We must act quickly, for the night is three-fourths gone, and with the daylight the sabits will be astir and our difficulties will be great."

Oro and four other men were detailed to search the passageways and, after five men had been selected for Vernia, Grandon led the others along the passageway through which he had first entered the subterranean chambers. On the way he collected a number of spears from the silent guardsmen.

With the assistance of his men he cut notches in the handles of four spears, chopped several others into shorter pieces, and with strips of the food sack for fastenings, constructed a serviceable ladder to reach the hole through which he had fallen.

He stationed three men at the foot of the ladder, instructing them as to their duties, and led the others up into the fungi storage room where he found things as he had left them. Very quietly they made their way to the dormitories where two hundred slaves were quartered, one man being left at the top of the ladder and another stationed at the entrance to the storage room.

Two soldier sabits were on guard without the main entrance to the dormitories. Grandon quietly stationed four of his men within and then began the business of awakening the slaves and sending them into the chamber below where three men waited to outfit them with armor and weapons and instruct them as to the correct method for dispatching sabits.

At dawn, just as the last of the men had been sent below, the sabit guards entered for the purpose of arousing the slaves. One was hacked to pieces as he came in the doorway, but the other, seeing the fate of its companion, escaped to warn the community.

Grandon now had an army of two hundred and twenty-three men, more than enough to guard the doorways. Though the sabits attacked desperately all morning long, he succeeded in keeping them at bay.

It was nearly midday before Oro reported to his commander. He did not arrive empty-handed, however, as his men staggered under the weight of four sets of sabit fetters. They had found many new wonders in their explorations of the subterranean passageways — great dining halls; barracks for soldiers; kitchens with cooking utensils and fireplaces; treasure vaults filled with jewels and precious metals; armories with weapons, armor and strange engines of war; bedrooms with grotesque but artistically constructed sleeping shelves and furniture, and a great throne room decorated in barbaric magnificence.

Grandon was greatly interested but he had business at hand that would brook no waiting.

The structure in which the king and queen sabits of the white community were quartered had but one entrance on the ground floor; there were, however, four runways connecting with its underground level which branched out at right angles, leading to other buildings of the community. His first problem, therefore, was to block these runways with warriors, thus cutting off the sabit rulers from these avenues of escape.

One of the four runways led directly under the dormitory and storeroom building occupied by Grandon and his men. This was already blocked with armed guards.

Another runway led to the sleeping quarters of the women and children in connection with which there was another storeroom. The third led to the building in which the women sorted sabit eggs and cared for the young fantas, while the fourth connected with the building in which the men looked after the larger fantas.

Sabit soldiers and workers used the last-named building for sleeping quarters, as well as the central structure. The green creatures were kept in the upper levels of the great central building, for the sabits had learned by experience that they all died in great numbers when quartered on the ground or under it. The mating pens were kept entirely separate from the rest of the buildings.

Leaving fifty men to guard the building which was in their possession, Grandon sallied forth at the head of his army. With Oro the Mighty on his right, and Tholto on his left, he fought at the head of his men for more than an hour before the attacking sabits gave way. These retreated to the central building, but Grandon was not ready to attack this. The women's quarters were captured in a relatively short time.

Leaving a guard of twenty-five armored men here, they attacked the building in which the women worked. Here they met with desperate resistance, and when finally they broke into it, found that the sabits had transported all eggs and young fantas to the central building.

After leaving twenty-five men to guard this building, they attacked the one in which the larger fantas were kept, but found it deserted.

Another guard of twenty-five was posted at this point, and now, with all avenues of escape blocked, they were ready to lay siege to the main structure. After posting guards at the various points the army numbered only ninety-eight men. With these he surrounded the structure, and attempted to battle his way through the narrow doorway.

This, he soon found, would be a well-nigh endless task, for two soldier sabits could hold back a regiment here, and although they were cut down time and again, others rushed in to take their place.

"If we only had a cannon of some sort," thought Grandon. Then he remembered the airship and the mattorks. Leaving Oro in charge of the besiegers with instructions to keep up the attack on the entrance, he took a dozen men and made for the tree in which the craft was jammed. While six of the men stood guard at the foot of the tree, he and the other six removed their armor and climbed up the rough bark.

They found the craft apparently undisturbed. With the aid of tools which he took from one of the drawers in the cab, he removed the three mattorks and, binding each to a man with a strip of sacking, he bade them convey them to the ground. He and the others followed with the ammunition, tools, searchlights, and whatever else looked useful. After donning their armor they returned to the attack.

As his men were unskilled in the use of the mattork, Grandon mounted only one weapon. Then he recalled his men from the doorway and began the bombardment, using explosive metal bullets. Only a few shots were required to enlarge the opening to the size of a dozen doorways and at the same time clear the surrounding space of sabits.

Grandon knew that the quarters of the queen and king sabit were in a central chamber on the ground floor, and that four walls intervened between this chamber, which was reached by winding passageways, and the outer opening. Moving his mattork closer, he shot down the second, third and fourth walls, while his warriors kept the sabits back.

Then he led a swift charge on the rulers of the white sabits, following by Oro and the men who carried the manacles.

It was here that he learned a peculiar characteristic of the king and queen sabits, for though the soldier and worker sabits retreated, the sabit rulers showed no disposition to do so. They appeared to have a certain standard of royal dignity which they punctiliously observed. They struggled desperately but unavailingly until the manacles were clamped in place. Then the white sabits became the slaves of men, for as soon as their rulers were made prisoners, all surrendered docilely.

Placing a guard of twenty-five men around the royal prisoners the Earthman ordered that the community life of the former masters of men be resumed. The fantas and eggs were returned to their respective buildings and the green creatures were conveyed to their leafy pastures — but this time the work was done entirely by the sabits. Later, when the community of marsh-people were organized, it was Grandon's plan that the sabits should fetch and carry for those who once served them.

When he returned to the dormitories, Grandon found Vernia in earnest and animated conversation with a young slave girl. Oro, who entered behind him, raised his visor at sight of the girl and the two embraced in a transport of joyous recognition.

"The girl is Rotha, a former slave of the brown-mouthed sabits," explained Vernia. "She has just escaped, and brings terrible tidings. This is Grandon of Terra, Rotha — the man of whom I told you. Let him hear your message at once."

"Today while working with the others," said Rotha, "I heard the rumor that the eighteen girls whom you left in the mating pens would be tortured to death before the other slaves tonight."

"But I saw no girls in the mating pens," said Grandon.

"Nor did I," answered Vernia. "Rotha says they had been taken to the inner rooms before I arrived."

Grandon swung on Oro. "Why didn't you tell me of this? We could have brought them with us.

The big marsh-man hung his head. "I thought you knew," he said. "You were in command, and I did not doubt that if you wished them brought with us you would say so. Every evening there are girls in the mating pens."

"Where are they to be punished?" asked Grandon.

"All the slaves will be herded before the hut of the queen sabit."

"Yes."

"Then each girl will be fed, feet first, to a large fanta."

"Can nothing be done to save them?" asked Vernia.

"We will do our best," Grandon replied. "Oro, assemble a hundred men at once."

CHAPTER XII

From among the hundred warriors marshaled by Oro, Grandon selected five who appeared above the average in intelligence, to act as officers, each to command nineteen men.

Absolute silence was observed as they marched. The Earthman led the column, followed by Oro with twenty men with two sets of sabit-fetters. After this group came the next officer whose crew carried a mattork, a rough tripod that Grandon had made for it, and ammunition. The others brought up the rear.

It was not until they arrived at a point near the mating pens that they saw the torches which had been planted before the central building. The doomed girls were huddled in a little group near the doorway, guarded by a dozen soldier sabits.

The king sabit stood in the glare of the torchlight, but his mate was not in sight. The female slaves and their children sat on the ground facing the entrance. Behind him stood the men, while soldier sabits formed a great circle about the whole scene.

Grandon saw two worker sabits pilot a huge fanta through the doorway. This lusty infant was larger even than the soldier sabits, almost ready to spin its cocoon. It gnashed it huge mandibles continuously, and wiggled from side to side, nearly upsetting its pilots with each jerk.

"We must work fast," said Grandon, "if we would be in time. The plan is as follows. Oro will take twenty men and the larger set of fetters and circle, coming up behind the buildings. When he hears the report of the mattork, he is to cut a door in the rear of the building, go immediately to the chamber of the queen sabit and make her prisoner.

"You two will take your detail and go with Oro's men to the rear of the building. Upon the second report of the mattork, one detail will charge around the right side of the building and fetter the king sabit while the other charges around the left side and rescues the girls, placing a guard around them.

"The fourth detail will go to a place behind that large surface root to the north of the sabits, while the last one will hide behind the mating pens on the south. At the third report of the mattork they will rush in and surround the slaves assembled before the building."

"But you thus will be left alone," remonstrated Oro. "The sabits will overpower and kill you, for you cannot resist an army single-handed."

"Have no fear for me," replied Grandon. "Only do as you are

bidden. Go now, swiftly and silently as possible. There is no time to lose."

In a moment Grandon was left entirely alone. He quickly mounted the mattork, meanwhile watching the ceremonies of the sabits from time to time. The king sabit had come out in front of the hungry fanta and was haranguing the slaves in the tone-language, no doubt warning them that if any of their number should even attempt to escape, a fate similar to that which was to be meted out to the girls awaited them.

After droning out his warnings for a full ten minutes the king sabit stepped to one side, whereupon four worker sabits seized a girl, two on a side, and carried her before the fanta.

Grandon quickly withdrew the clip of explosive bullets he had in the mattork and inserted one of solid missiles instead. The girl was being pushed feet foremost toward those gaping jaws, and although he knew Oro would not be ready, he took careful aim at the hideous head.

Just as he was ready to press the button the form of a man appeared on the direct line between the mattork and target. Grandon lifted his tripod, intending to try a shot from another position, when he saw the man who had momentarily saved the fanta's life hurl a huge rock fragment straight for its ugly head. The missile struck the mark squarely, and the great soft-bodied monster, after a convulsive shudder, sank over on its side, stone dead.

Once more Grandon put his clip of explosive bullets in the mattork. He saw the man turn and dodge among the snapping sabits; he succeeded in breaking through the line and in keeping a short distance ahead of his pursuers.

Training his weapon on those sabits immediately behind the fugitive, the Earthman opened fire. The exploding missile tore a great gap in the ranks of the monsters, killing a half dozen and disabling as many more, whereupon the others paused, running this way and that in their endeavor to locate the unseen attacker.

Suddenly Grandon leaped up on the surface root behind him and, turning his pocket flashlight on himself, shouted defiance to the sabits in the tone-language. The king sabit saw him almost immediately, and vibrated his antennae excitedly, whereupon all but a dozen soldier sabits who remained to guard the slaves charged down on Grandon. As he leaped back to the ground and made his mattork ready, the man who had broken through the sabit guards arrived, panting heavily.

"Give me a weapon," cried the stranger, "and I will fight with you."

Grandon handed him the spiked club. "Hit them between the eyes," he said. "It is the only vulnerable spot. If you are as skillful with a club as you are at hurling stones, I am sure you will account for a few of them."

The newcomer smiled slightly. He was evidently not a marshman, for his features were clean-cut, his hair a light golden yellow. He walked with the carriage of a soldier.

"It was a lucky hit," he replied. "Throwing stones is not my specialty. I could do much better with that weapon."

Grandon fired the signal for the second attack.

"Where did you learn to use the mattork?" Grandon asked his ally.

"I was captain in the army of Mernerum for several years, and was credited with being a fairly good marksman."

"Here, then, take the weapon. Let me see what you can do with it. The next shot will be the final signal for my men. See if you can stop the charge of these soldier sabits."

The newcomer grasped the weapon with the assurance of a master musician taking up his instrument. The first shot was a direct hit in the foremost ranks of the sabits, and thereafter he fired with unerring accuracy. It was but one weapon against an army, however, and both men knew that in a few seconds they would be overwhelmed.

Grandon saw one crew of armored men struggling to fetter the king sabit, while another group struck down the guards surrounding the girls. Before the last two details had come to blows with the other guards, the mattork-tripod was knocked over by the charging monsters, and both men were fighting with their backs against the thick surface root, Grandon swinging his heavy axe while his newfound ally used the spiked club almost as skillfully as he had used the mattork.

Closer and closer pressed the sabits, snapping their mighty forceps which were easily capable of cutting the unarmored men in two with one nip. The newcomer knew this, yet he laughed as he fought, and at times taunted the furious attackers in the tone-language.

"You jest with death, yet fight with the fury of a cornered lion," said Grandon. "What is your name?"

"I am called Joto, which in the language of the Mernerum means 'The Merry One.' Take that!" crushing the skull of a huge sabit, "thou self-styled master of men! Names matter but little now, for we have not long to live; yet I would not die without knowing the name of the mighty fighter to whom I owe the few moment of life I have remaining."

"I am Grandon of Terra," answered the Earthman, cleaving the head of an antagonist and leaping back to avoid the snap of another. He tried to wrench the axe free, but it stuck, and the next moment powerful forceps encircled him.

With a final tug at the handle of his weapon, he was jerked from the side of his companion and mauled about by a dozen sabits who alternately shook him, crunched him with their mandibles, and tried to pull him to pieces. The armor held, but the man inside it was swiftly lapsing into unconsciousness.

A powerful sabit, more cunning than its comrades, seized Grandon by the ankles and beat him against the hard surface root. At the second terrific shock the thread of consciousness snapped asunder.

CHAPTER XIII

Returning consciousness brought numerous twinges of pain to Grandon. He stirred uneasily. A soft hand pressed his fevered brow, and a sweet voice said: "Speak not so loudly, Rotha. You will awaken him and he needs rest — much rest and quiet."

Slowly he opened his eyes. He was lying on a sleeping shelf that projected in a half-moon shape from the wall like the nest of a cave-swallow. At the foot of his couch, which was of stone but lined with soft moss, Rotha, the slave girl, held a golden vessel in which was a pasty compound of aromatic herbs, while Vernia occupied a place at the head. His armor had been removed and his bruises covered with the sweet-smelling ointment.

In the center of the room a guard stood stiffly erect, holding a sputtering torch, by the light of which he could see grotesquely carved figures on the walls, a queer table shaped like a great tortoise and chairs that were human figures seated on round pedestals, the body forming the back, the lap the seat, and outstretched arms with hands bent downward and fingertips touching the thighs forming the arm rests.

The furniture was all cut from hard wood of a reddish purple color and highly polished. The floor was of hexagonal blocks of varicolored stone and presented a smooth, glossy surface.

He saw all these things at a glance, then his eyes sought those of the girl at his bedside. "It is indeed an honor to be nursed by the greatest ruler in all Zarovia," he said, smiling feebly.

"I'm afraid it is but small recompense for your services," she replied. "Besides, I am a ruler no longer, nor is it probable that I ever will be again. Within fifty-eight days my cousin Prince Destho will assume the crown. I am sure he must have been the instigator of my abduction. My legal right to the throne will have been forever forfeited. I will have been away from the capital for a year, and such is the inexorable law."

"Surely you must be mistaken in your calculations. I am positive you have not been away from Reabon for over half a year at most."

"You forget that you are on Zarovia, where the years are much shorter than on your planet. Our world is closer to the sun than yours, consequently our year is only two hundred and twenty-five days in length."

"That's true. Then we must start for Reabon at once . . ."

"But how? The marsh-men say there is no way out of this valley but a secret tunnel, known only to the sabits; and this is said to be guarded night and day by a huge army of soldier sabits, recruited from all the communities in the valley."

"But does not the river cut through the surrounding cliffs on its way to the sea?"

"I am told that the river ends in a great whirlpool a few miles from here. They say it falls into a bottomless pit, for the pit has never been known to fill up or the river to overflow its banks."

"Then, we have the alternative of scaling the cliffs, or finding the secret passageway of the sabits and fighting our way through," said Grandon. "In either event we must start quickly, for the time is short."

Despite her protests Grandon arose, gritting his teeth as pain shot through his body. While he donned his armor with the assistance of the two girls he learned that all of the slaves had been rescued and the king and queen sabits were prisoners.

Joto had escaped his pursuers and personally led a party to the rescue of Grandon. They took him to Vernia, who had him conveyed to this bedchamber of an ancient Albine ruler, where she and Rotha nursed him all through the night.

Grandon was drawing on his gauntlets when Oro entered. At sight of his commander, Oro saluted smartly, after the style of soldiers of Zarovian empires.

"Where did you learn the military salute, and why are you here instead of guarding the roga-sabit as instructed?" asked Grandon.

"We have been taught many things by Joto, who has assumed temporary command of your army," replied Oro. "He has set the other captains you appointed to the tasks of guarding the king and queen sabits of the two communities, drilling, and learning the meaning of military orders. In addition he has been training a crew of thirty men to handle the mattorks. We are in grave danger, for the sabits of all the communities, realizing that we menace their safety, have united with the common purpose of annihilating us. Our scouts report the marshaling of a mighty force in the red-mouthed community, which they have made their base of operations. Joto thinks they will attack us before nightfall."

"Joto has commendable initiative and ability to match it," said Grandon. "Let us go and see what he has accomplished."

Accompanied by the two girls, they made their way to the place where Grandon had fallen into the passageway; the whole had been widened and a broad stairway constructed. Two guards saluted stiffly as they passed.

They found Joto outside the structure, supervising the practice of the mattork crew, who used empty bullets and gas clips but went through the motions of loading, aiming and firing with surprising speed and precision, while four units of a hundred men each were being drilled by their officers. He turned and raised his visor with a welcoming salute as Grandon and the others approached.

"I see that you have considerable military genius," said Grandon.

"Having trained men in the art of warfare for some time, I should be proficient," said Joto. "However, I bow to you as a superior strategist. The attack you planned against the brown-mouthed sabits was marvelously conceived and executed. We await your orders."

"How many sabits do you expect will attack us?"

"Twenty thousand, at the very least. Every community is sending no less than a hundred, and there are more than two hundred communities."

"Twenty thousand sabits," mused Grandon. "Enough to sweep us away bodily, and these building with us."

"Easily."

"With four hundred and fifty men it will be impossible to guard both communities, or even all the buildings of one community. Have the brown-mouthed sabit rulers brought to the central building of this community, and there kept with the rulers of the white community. Withdraw our guards from all other buildings, and block all the runways with stones except the one which leads here from the central building."

"Then we may as well kill all of our sabit slaves at once," said Joto, "for the attackers will surely kill them."

"Why should they war on their own kind," asked Grandon, "when it is their purpose to rescue them?"

"Their purpose is not altruistic, but protective only. As our slaves, the brown-mouthed and the white sabits are enemies of their kind. Moreover, they will fight to protect their rulers, their eggs and their fantas."

"Why not let them fight?" asked Vernia. "They should account for a few of the attackers."

"Right," exclaimed Grandon. "Leave them to guard the brown-mouthed community and the three outer structures of this one. No doubt they will all be killed in the first charge, but it is probable they will account for an equal number of enemies."

Joto sent a messenger to order the brown-mouthed rulers brought to new quarters, as directed by Grandon. It was decided that a hundred men should be posted in the central building, with one mattork placed on the roof. The other two mattorks would command the battlefield from a place on the roof of the men's sleeping quarters.

The stores of dried fungi from both communities were removed from their storage rooms and carried to the subterranean chambers, as were also hundreds of sacks of the sticky food. While Joto supervised this work, Grandon took Oro and a crew of twenty-five men to examine the engines of war in the ancient armory of the Albines, which Oro had discovered while exploring the underground passageways.

The huge subterranean armory, next to the throne room, was the largest excavation in the entire system. Its floor level was considerably below that of the passageways and its ceiling was higher and dome-shaped. Though the floor was of hard granite, the walls and ceiling were as elaborately decorated as those of the fountain room, the reliefs being almost exclusively battle scenes between Albines and sabits, and in many cases showing in operation engines of war similar to those which stood about on the floor.

Grandon examined the heavy, death-dealing instruments. Most of them were better for attack on the sabit dwellings than for defense.

There were catapults that hurled huge stones or fired long, heavy, metal-tipped missiles which acted as battering rams. There were instruments apparently adapted to the spraying of poisonous liquids, though no ammunition for them could be found.

Among the devices which required considerable mechanical ingenuity were queer three-wheeled carts built in the shape of hollow triangles, the outside edges of which were protected by curved blades and spiked clubs that whirled rapidly when the machines were pushed forward by men running inside. A small group of men operating on level ground might cut a path through an entire sabit army with one of these machines.

Having sent Oro and his men to Joto with six of the carts, Grandon was examining the brown metal spring of one of the catapults when his attention was attracted by a curiously wrought cabinet standing against the wall. What he at first took to be narrow sliding drawers proved to be thin flat slabs of stone on which designs had been scratched with some stone instrument. The topmost slab was covered with a carefully drafted design of an Albine catapult. The next illustrated the construction and working principles of the spraying machines.

As he pulled out slab after slab he found plans for the construction of practically all the machines he had seen, but the bottom slab consisted of two maps side by side, the general shape of both being identical, but the details different.

He recognized one as a map of the valley surface, the other as a plan of the underground passageways and chambers of the Albines.

A careful scrutiny of the surface map revealed only the solid, unbroken cliffs in oval formation, so he concluded that the tunnel mentioned by the marsh-men must not have been known to the Albines. Turning from this to the underground map, he noticed a discrepancy that had previously escaped his observation, for in the first map the river began at the western end of the valley and wound its way south of the center to the point where it ended in a whirl-pool; while in the second it began in the northwest and flowed for some distance north of the center, apparently going directly through the point where the other map showed the whirlpool, and flowing thence on through the cliffs to the east.

Grandon had seen enough of the valley to know that but one river flowed through it. Obviously it was an underground river! Furthermore, it could not have been mapped unless navigable, in which case it offered a means of escape from the valley.

He noticed that at one point the river appeared to touch the end of the chamber he was in, but there seemed to be no mode of exit other than the door which he had entered. He walked back and forth along the walls searching for a concealed door.

When about to give up his seemingly hopeless quest he arrived at a certain point where his attention was attracted by a gentle mur-muring as of distant waters. Pausing, he listened breathlessly, and noticed that the sound seemed to emanate from the figure of an armed warrior which was chiseled in bold relief on the wall before him.

A careful search revealed a small lever behind the right elbow, and on pulling this section of the wall four feet wide and higher than a man moved toward him, revealing a flat platform and a flight of steps beyond. The sound of roaring water was now plainly audible.

Grandon stepped on the platform and, finding it firm, held his torch aloft and descended the steps. After traveling for a consider-able distance he reached a level floor of stone and a moment later came upon a great stone dock on which, as far as his torchlight car-ried in both directions, reposed a fleet of metal boats. Each was about fifty feet in length and built in the form of those huge am-phibious reptiles such as he had rescued Vernia from, back in Reabon. The prow ended in an arched serpentine neck and head, while the stern terminated in the flat, pointed tail. Behind these grotesque craft he could see the black, foam-flecked water rushing headlong beneath stalactite-festooned subterranean arches.

He examined one of the boats. It was constructed of brown metal similar to that from which the Albines made their weapons and armor, and appeared quite strong and seaworthy. The deck was completely arched over with the same material, fashioned in imitation of reptilian scales, except at the front and rear where there were oval holes provided with hinged metal lids.

Upon entering the forward hole he found a roomy interior all of metal, and saw that the hull was rigidly ribbed and braced. Twenty large metal paddles lay on the floor and there were twenty seats for paddlers, ten on each side, while metal hoods projected outward, almost to the water line, in such a manner that they would completely hide the paddlers and protect them from the missiles of an enemy. The steering device and helmsman's seat were immediately behind the top of the rear entrance hole, and were also protected by movable metal plates.

Upon his moving the tiller the entire tail turned; the rudder was fastened beneath the tail.

Grandon made his way back to the armory and carefully closed the secret doorway. He started along the passageway, when he noticed a soldier running toward him.

The man stopped suddenly when he saw Grandon and saluted stiffly. "Joto bade me tell you that the sabits are beginning to attack."

"Attacking already?" Grandon hurried to join in the momentous conflict which was to decide, once and for all, whether men or monsters should rule the Valley of the Sabits.

As soon as he had left the room, a tall, bulky figure in armor stepped from behind a large catapult and went directly to the hidden door, wrenching one of the torches from its fastening as he passed. The soldier fumbled with the hidden lever for a moment, then managed to swing the door back and disappeared in the dark interior.

Some twenty minutes later he reappeared, carefully fastened the door and replaced the torch. His visor was raised; the face was that of Tholto.

"A way out of the valley," he muttered. "I have only to gather a few provisions and to get *her*."

CHAPTER XIV

The pandemonium of battle was punctuated by the staccato reports of the men's cannon-like mattocks as Grandon reached the interior of the men's sleeping quarters. He mounted to the topmost chamber from which Joto directed the activities of the two mattork crews while he shouted orders to the defenders.

Here he found Vernia and Rotha. "See," the marsh-girl cried, "they come by thousands and tens of thousands. They cover the entire landscape. Our defenses will be crushed."

"You forget that they are only brutes, Rotha," replied Vernia, "and as such may be overcome by creatures of superior intellect. Men are the lords of creation, not sabits."

"But they are wiser than all other animals . . ."

"Except men." She turned to Grandon smiling. "We are going to win this battle, are we not, Robert Grandon?"

"Most assuredly," he replied. "However, I am not so positive that we will be able to hold this building. This is hardly a safe place."

"You forget," said Vernia, "that I, too, am a soldier. I prefer to remain here, and if necessary, take part in the fighting."

"I am sure you are too good a soldier to disobey orders, and I am in command. You are ordered below."

A quick flash of resentment came to her eyes at his tone and words.

"You presume to command me? To dictate to the Princess of Reabon? I only command. Others obey."

In outraged dignity she turned and started toward the ramparts, but a strong pair of arms picked her up and carried her down the runways and to the foot of the stairway, while Rotha trailed behind. Grandon set Vernia gently down and, taking her by the shoulder, turned her so she looked up at him with flaming eyes and heaving bosom.

"You would only be in my way, and would more than likely be carried off by the sabits. Now will you go forward peaceably, or must I carry you the rest of the way?"

A slight flush suffused her cheeks, but when she raised her eyes to his, there was a new look in them. "I will go, my commander."

"Spoken like a true soldier." He paused for a moment to admire her, walking gracefully with Rotha down the passageway; then he turned to get back to the fighting.

Grandon found the lower floor of the men's sleeping quarters well defended, so climbed once more to the top of the structure where Joto was directing the battle. As far as he could see in every direction the ground swarmed with sabits. In a short time the brown-mouthed sabit community was overwhelmed and its buildings razed to the ground, as were three of the outer structures of the white sabit community.

The men in the central building held their own for a considerable time, but their outer ring of sabit guards were killed and torn to pieces almost instantly. At length it appeared inevitable that this building must fall. Sabits were gnawing their way through the walls and more and more soldiers were required to hold them back.

"I will take a force to help them," said Joto.

"No. You are doing very well here. I will go to their assistance," replied Grandon.

Taking fifty men from the reserve force in the storeroom Grandon led them through the low underground runway. As they arrived the guards were being driven to the inner chambers, but they rallied with the aid of the new reinforcements and once more drove the sabits from the building.

Sheb, the captain in command here, was on the roof directing the mattork crew, so Grandon climbed thither after assuring himself that the first floor was well defended. He found the crew standing idle while Sheb, fuming and cursing, was attempting to dislodge a jammed gas clip from the breech of the weapon.

"Are you all so witless that you insert a clip backward after having been told the proper way a thousand times?" he roared. "For the price of a bowl of wine I would have you stripped of your armor and thrown to the sabits."

"Let me try," said Grandon coolly. "I believe I can get that clip out for you."

Surprise at the sudden appearance of his commander, Sheb stood up and saluted hurriedly. With the point of his sword Grandon gently pried the recalcitrant clip, turned it, and closed the breech. Once more the crew sprayed bullets into the ranks of the attackers.

A soldier rushed up from below. "The outer walls are nearly gone," he gasped. "In a few minutes the building will cave in."

"Order a retreat. There is no use in defending this shell."

"The king and queen sabit prisoners — shall we take them with us?"

"Leave them behind."

"If we leave them we will have no sabit slaves," said Sheb.

"Plenty more can be captured if we successfully withstand this attack," replied Grandon.

Another messenger arrived from below.

"The sabits have burrowed into the runway," he cried. We will not be able to return to the other building."

"Everyone below at once," shouted Grandon. "Bring the mattork and ammunition. Hurry!"

The building trembled and one of the walls collapsed as they rushed to the ground floor. "Into the runway, every man of you," he commanded. "Let the mattork crew go first and clear the way."

Soon the men were all crowded into the narrow runway while Grandon and Sheb, standing abreast, fought off the sabits that attempted to follow. The entire structure collapsed a few minutes later, crushing not only the imprisoned sabit rulers but many of the attackers as well. The entrance to the runway was completely bottled up by fallen debris.

Shouldering his way through his crowded soldiers, Grandon at length arrived at the point where the sabits had burrowed into the runway. Here the mattork crew worked desperately, flanked by a half dozen soldiers. The cut in the runway was more than twenty feet across, and swarmed with sabits. Across this breach he could see Oro and his men fighting to keep the attackers from entering on the other side.

Meanwhile the sabits on the ground above the runways were burrowing in a hundred places. Already a third of the men who guarded the central building had been dragged away by the attackers.

After a short conversation with the captain Sheb, Grandon ran across the twenty-foot breach the sabits had made in their defenses, leaping this way and that to avoid the snapping forceps.

Oro and the others welcomed him with enthusiasm.

He ran swiftly through the passageway and, upon coming up, quickly placed crews in the ancient Albine fighting chariots he had sent from the armory some time before. Taking a place with the men in the foremost machine, he led them through the door straight into the army of sabits, the guards standing aside to let them pass. They formed a flying wedge with Grandon's machine at the apex, cutting a wide swath in the ranks of the attackers.

The efficacy of the machines was surprising, even to Grandon, who had formed some idea of their possibilities. The whirling knives and clubs literally cut the opposing sabits to ribbons.

Arriving at the mouth of the runway which held the imprisoned men, they quickly drove back the attackers, then kept them at bay by running a circle about the breach while Sheb led his followers to safety. When the last man had crossed they formed a wedge once more and cut their way back to their comrades, entering the door amid shouts of acclamation from the defenders.

Night fell, and the fighting continued by torchlight, while Grandon made further plans. There were more than a hundred of the machines in the armory, and he planned to press them all into service as soon as possible. Taking the entire force of reserves with him, he hurried thither, not noticing the absence of Vernia and Rotha, who he supposed had retired to their bedchambers in the women's quarters.

He was surprised at sight of the open exit door, but decided that he must not have pushed it far enough for the lock to catch.

The machines were quickly dragged from their ancient resting places and provided with crews. Within a half hour they were assembled in the building, ready for the charge. One by one they emerged from the doorway, spreading out in a great line six hundred feet long, then "Forward!" shouted Grandon, while Joto on the roof withheld the mattork fire.

The charge was irresistible. With every fifty feet of progress a thousand sabits perished. They cut completely through the sabit army, turned their machines and charged again, breaking down the resistance of those who had instinctively filled in the lines. Back and forth they drove through the thinning ranks of the attackers until the survivors, seeing that further resistance was futile, turned and fled.

Thus was the power of the sabits forever broken in the valley.

When Grandon entered the building with his victorious machine crews, the people cheered until they were hoarse. Posting a guard at the entrance, he called them to attend what he had to say to them in the great audience chamber of the ancient Albines.

When the people were assembled in the audience chamber, Grandon mounted the steps of the throne and faced them.

"My friends," he began, "I have called you together, not merely to congratulate you on your momentous victory over those monsters who have, for centuries, oppressed you and your forefathers, but also to make a few suggestions for your coming nation. For countless ages you have been ruled by the sabits. From now on you will need a government of your own. As you have no royal family, you must choose your king. Let him be one who has your interest at heart, one who has the ability and the will to carry forward the great work which has only begun tonight. Whom will you have for king?"

"Grandon of Terra!" shouted a burly soldier, waving his sword a lot. Immediately the cry was reechoed throughout the audience.

He held up his hand for silence, but many minutes elapsed

before the tumult subsided. "I appreciate the honor," he said, "and regret that I must decline it. It is of vital importance that the Princess of Reabon be returned to her country and friends at once. Moreover, my own kingdom of Uxpo awaits a ruler.

"If you will permit me to make a suggestion, I will name one who is admirably suited for the place. One who, by his military genius, and training, his bravery and prowess as a soldier, has already won a place at the head of your army. Let Joto be your first king."

Joto was not without considerable popularity, and so when Grandon led him up the steps to the throne, there was a burst of cheering almost equal to that which had followed the nomination of Grandon. Grandon took the crown of the ancient Albine rulers, blew the dust of centuries from it, and placed it on the bared head of the young commander.

"You have elected me king," said Joto with his inevitable smile, "but king of what? Just as truly as we were people without a country before our deliverance, so now we are a country without a name. My first official act, therefore, will be to name this nation, Granterra, in grateful tribute to the man who has made it possible."

There was more cheering for Grandon, for Joto and for the newly-named nation. Then Joto, after making Oro commander, appointed the five councilors who were to assist him, asking them to step forward as their names were called. He named the four other captains and Tholto in order, but Tholto failed to appear.

One of the latter's lieutenants, on being questioned, stated that Tholto had left him in command during the hottest fighting, and had departed with twenty men. About this time, Grandon recalled that he had not seen either Vernia or Rotha since he left them at the foot of the stairway, and hastily sent a girl to the women's quarters to ascertain if they were safe. Joto dispatched soldiers to search all the underground passageways and rooms for the missing mojak and his men.

While they were out, the girl Grandon had sent returned with the news that neither Vernia nor Rotha had been seen since morning.

In a flash Grandon thought of the open door he had noticed while getting the fighting machines; he rushed out of the audience chamber and along the passageway which led to the armory. Joto, Oro and the more swift-footed among the soldiers followed closely.

Quickly springing the hidden catch, he ran down the steps and out on the docks where he saw at a glance that one of the boats was missing.

"You may as well call in your searchers, Joto," he said sadly. "They are gone."

"But where — how?"

"This stream leads out of the valley. They have disappeared. One of the boats is missing. The conclusion is obvious. I must have twenty picked fighting men at once, provisions, water, torches, and a mattork cannon. And, Oro, get me one of those large searchlights we took from the airship. We will need it in these caverns. Hurry!"

While Grandon carefully examined the nearest boat to determine its seaworthiness, Joto rushed his men as they had never been rushed before. Within a half hour the craft was provisioned and fitted with searchlight and mattork, while twenty of Granterra's brawniest fighting men stood ready to man her.

Grandon said good-by to Joto and turning to Oro, was surprised to find him in an attitude of supplication.

"A boon, mighty Grandon of Terra," he pleaded.

"Gladly, Oro, if within my power."

"Take me with you."

"I have twenty men already, and don't want to weigh the boat unnecessarily. Besides you are now commander-in-chief of Granterra's armies, and your duty lies here. Why do you wish to leave?"

"Tholto has stolen one who means more than life to me. I would rescue her or avenge her."

"You mean Rotha?"

Oro nodded.

"Ask King Joto. If you have his consent, you may come."

"You have my consent, Oro, and both of you my heartfelt wishes for your success," said Joto. "I will appoint a substitute for Oro while he is gone, and will see that he is reinstated on his return."

The soldiers took their places at the paddle holes, Oro was placed at the tiller, and Grandon manned the searchlight on the forward deck. A hundred willing hands pushed them off, and they forged swiftly ahead beneath the eroded archways hung with glistening stalactites.

Grandon found Oro a skillful navigator and his soldiers adept with the paddles. Joto had selected them, not only for their fighting prowess, but also because they had previously lived with their people in the great salt marsh where boats were a necessity and every man proficient in their use.

The stream gradually widened as they progressed, and often forked in numerous ramifications, flowing through a labyrinth of arched caves for a distance, then uniting in a common channel farther on. The waters and the banks on either side of them teemed with weird subterranean life. Reptiles and animals of a thousand sizes and kinds swarmed the banks, and glided through the water about the boat.

Once they stuck a huge saurian that nearly capsized their craft, but the creature sank out of sight and did not offer to molest them. Grandon noticed one peculiarity common to all, namely, that they were sightless, and paid no attention to the searchlight. In fact, most of them were without even rudimentary eyes, though a few had eye-sockets, and one or two boasted antennae-like feelers sprouting from the head.

Upon rounding a sharp bend in the river they suddenly heard a terrific roaring sound that totally obliterated the noise made by the stream. Grandon flashed his light ahead to learn the cause, then quickly ordered the paddlers to reverse, for directly ahead was a solid wall of falling water that churned the stream into foam and sent clouds of spray whirling toward them.

The momentum of the boat carried them dangerously close before they could stop, but Oro veered to one side, ramming the prow against the bank until the paddlers could make headway against the current. When at a safe distance they turned and made for the first fork, through which they found a safe passage around the falls.

That the wall of water they had so narrowly escaped was at the bottom of the whirlpool in which the surface stream ended, Grandon could not doubt. He was therefore able to determine their distance from the cliffs with reasonable certainty, and calculated that within two hours at the most, they should be outside the valley.

He stood on the deck of the swiftly-gliding boat, turning his light this way and that, watching the blind monsters, and did not see the crouching thing on the top of the great overhanging shelf under which they must shortly pass — a thing without eyes, but with nose and ears abnormally developed, a thing with great cavernous jaws armed with a dozen row of razor-sharp teeth and with powerful claws that could rend and tear the toughest saurians limb form limb.

It was all over in an instant. Oro, looking ahead as they came under the overhanging bank, saw a great, sinuous bulk shoot downward, sweeping Grandon from the narrow deck and into the dark depths below.

They stopped the boat and hung near the spot for more than an hour, hoping that Grandon might have broken away from the monster, but saw only a few bubbles and something that looked like blood, both of which quickly disappeared in the foaming current.

Frantically they sought him, making vain efforts to surmount the shelf and rescue their commander. At last, they sadly resumed their journey.

CHAPTER XV

For several hours after she was seized and bound by Tholto's men Vernia lay with Rotha in darkness in the bottom of the boat. She could not see the members of the crew on either side, though she heard the rhythmic strokes of the paddles and caught scraps of the conversation.

Tholto acted as helmsman, holding his torch aloft with one hand while he swung the tiller with the other. From time to time she caught the glint of torchlight as he stooped to issue hoarse commands.

It was by sheer luck that they happened on the channel which led them around the column of falling water. Several hours after they passed the falls, the interior of the boat was suddenly illuminated by daylight streaming through the front and rear entrance holes. After another hour of paddling Tholto placed one of his men at the helm and, untying the bonds of the two girls, put food and water before them.

He watched them silently while they drank — neither ate anything — then tied them once more and resumed his place on deck. The man who had acted as steersman distributed food and water to the others at their posts, half the men paddling while the other half ate and drank. Some time later — Vernia judged it to be about midday — the boat lurched violently, then settled down to a familiar, rolling motion that vividly reminded her of her trip with Grandon in the fragile toadstool.

Toward evening Tholto ordered half of the men on deck while the others redoubled their efforts at the paddles. In a few moments the keel grated sharply on gravel and the lurching ceased. Tholto threw Vernia over his shoulder as if she had been a sack of sabit food and carried her up on the bank while another of the men followed with Rotha.

The crew speedily unloaded, then dragged the lightened craft high on the bank. A fire was started in the lee of the rocky cliffs, and two of the men who had gone in search of meat returned with a large pink lizard which was cut up and roasted over the flames.

The cliff behind them was honeycombed with natural caves. Tholto chose the largest and best situated of these for himself, the next best for his men.

While the evening meal was being prepared, moss was gathered for couches by some, while others went in search of roots to make Zarovian wine. When the men had eaten their fill Tholto undid the bonds of both girls and ordered them to serve the kova. For cups they were provided with the shells of large bivalves. Rotha complied meekly, but Vernia refused with flashing eyes.

Tholto laughed. "I will tame you. Your lessons will start tonight."

Binding her hands and feet once more, despite her struggles, he carried her into the dark cave and threw her on the floor.

"Now lie there and reflect on the folly of resistance. Much good wine is being consumed, and I would not miss it. I will return presently, and if you so much as utter a whisper of protest, you will learn why strong men fear the wrath of Tholto."

Many of the marsh-men had not tasted liquor for years, each man's abstinence dating from the time he had been captured by the sabits. Small wonder, then, that they called for more and more. Tholto might have drunk to excess with the rest, had not other pleasures beckoned. As it was, he took only enough to intoxicate him slightly, then walked unsteadily into the cave where he had left Vernia bound and helpless.

Grandon's left arm was pinned to his body in the grip of powerful jaws that would have cut him in two had it not been for the armor, but the right arm was free; and drawing his sword, he plunged it again and again into the leathery throat.

He held his breath until it seemed that his lungs would burst, but the pressure of those jaws did not relax, and he prayed that his blade might find a vital spot before it was too late.

To his surprise, the water suddenly drained from his helmet and he tasted air. It was dank, foul air, charged with the offensive odor of putrefied flesh, but at that moment as welcome to his bursting lungs as a balmy, sweet-scented zephyr from a fern forest.

The monster ground his teeth ineffectually against Grandon's armor for a moment, then dropped him on a slimy floor and, putting its huge claw on his chest, gave vent to a horrible, gurgling roar.

The creature continued its disconsolate roaring, which was intensified a hundred-fold by ringing, cavernous echoes, and Grandon noticed that with each roar the gurgling sound seemed more pronounced and the vocal tones grew weaker. Slowly the weight on his chest relaxed — slowly the creature sank over on its side.

With a quick jerk he rolled from under the mighty claw in time to avoid the convulsive death struggles of the monster.

Taking his small flashlight from its pouch, Grandon surveyed the scene about him.

The lair of the great sightless carnivore was an arched cavern which ended at the water's edge in front of him and appeared to connect with a series of other caverns behind. As it was impossible for him to return under water the way he had come, Grandon turned his footsteps toward the caverns in the rear.

As he journeyed on and on through that intricate maze of dark, damp, dismal caves, it seemed that they only led him deeper into the bowels of the planet. Moisture dripped constantly from a thousand pendent, crystalline points overhead; presently, however, the floor slanted upward, the dripping ceased, and the puddles disappeared.

Quite suddenly and unexpectedly he emerged on the bank of a large stream. It looked like the one in which he had been plunged some time before, but he could not be certain.

What was that? Could it be that he saw a human being moving slowly along the bank, apparently plucking and eating small fungus growths? And there, farther on, was another, and yet another, until only a short distance from where he stood the bank literally swarmed with them.

The creatures paid no attention whatever to his flashlight. He turned it directly on the one nearest him and gasped in astonishment. It was manlike in form, but a grotesque caricature of the genus homo. It had long, bony webbed fingers and toes armed with sharp claws. The smooth, hairless skin was a mottled silver gray in color, like that of a mackerel. But the face — Grandon was positive he had never seen anything so hideous in all his Zarovian wanderings.

It consisted, in front, of a broad, flat nose, and a mouth filled with huge, rat-like teeth, and was minus chin, eyes or forehead. The hairless pate slanted straight back from the root of the nose and up from the base of the neck, ending in a conical point at he back. The ears were human in form, but easily four times as large as the aural appendages of any man Grandon had ever seen, and the creature kept them constantly in motion, presumably for the purpose of guarding against prowling enemies, or locating prey which it obviously could not see.

A stealthy sound behind him caused Grandon to wheel suddenly. There, not three feet from him, stood a creature similar to the one he had been watching. It sniffed the air in his direction for a moment with ears cocked sharply forward, then raised its head and uttered a long, mournful, wailing shriek.

Before he could sense the import of that cry he was surrounded by a chattering, excited group of creatures, seemingly materialized from the darkness around him. Grandon drew his sword and awaited the first act of hostility from that narrowing circle.

To his surprise, they made no move to attack him, but seemed only curious. One, a trifle bolder than the rest, reached out long bony fingers and touched his armor, then made a queer, cackling noise. Others, emboldened by the experiment of their comrade, pawed him over in turn, while the caverns rang with the echoes of their cackling.

Grandon grew tired of being manhandled, and attempted to push the things away from him with outstretched arms. They were apparently harmless, and he had not the heart to use his sword on them. He learned by mistake too late, for they took this movement as a sign of hostility, and a dozen of them pounced on him, bearing him to the floor, where, pinned beneath their combined weight, he could scarcely lift a finger.

Then, above the shrieking and chattering of his captors, he heard the familiar click of paddles against the metal sides of a boat. A bright beam of light flashed over him.

"Oro!" he shouted at the top of his voice. "To the rescue, Oro!"

Once more the ray of the searchlight played on the struggling mass of creatures. It hung there. A hoarse command sounded simultaneously with the noise of a hollow metal scraping on stone. Then there was the clank of armored men running, followed by the sound of blows and unearthly shrieks of anguish. Two stalwart marsh-men helped Grandon to his feet as the last of his captors fled off, howling in dismay.

There was a brief but joyous reunion of commander and men on the bank, which was rudely broken into by a shower of missiles from out of the darkness, hurled with uncanny accuracy. Nearly every man in the company was struck, and several bowled over, though their armor protected them from serious injury.

Grandon ordered everyone aboard, as he had no stomach for useless slaughter, and felt pity rather than animosity toward the sightless, feeble-minded creatures that had attacked him.

For some time after they pushed away from the shore, stones continued to rain against the boat and splash in the water about it, but on rounding a curve in the stream the shower of missiles ceased and they saw no more of the strange creatures who hurled them.

An hour later they emerged from beneath a perpendicular cliff into broad daylight, shot a swift rapids, and proceeded on a beautiful, sparkling stream, dotted with verdant islets and flanked on either side by the great salt marshes.

The ocean breeze kept cane brakes constantly in motion, producing an odd, rattling sound that had a peculiar, depressing effect on Grandon. It seemed that these weeds were conspiring against him as other forces had conspired, to keep Vernia from him. It was a relief when, toward evening, they reached the ocean coast and landed a short time to give the men a chance to stretch their cramped muscles and steep some liquor.

While they built a fire of dried reeds and prepared the roots, Grandon and Oro explored the coast for some distance southward without finding any sign of those whom they sought. They accordingly had four of the men paddle them across the mouth of the river and traversed the coastline looking for signs of a camp and a cooking fire, when the sharp-eyed Oro suddenly uttered an exclamation of surprise and ran down to the water's edge. Lying on the sand where it had been deposited by the breakers was an empty food sack.

"They came this way in the boat," he exclaimed.

They hurried back to the camp, and, after a hasty meal, embarked northward. The sudden, inky darkness of Venus descended before they had gone far, and the wind rose, making coastline travel exceedingly difficult. Toward midnight they sighted a flickering light ahead. On coming closer they saw a large campfire surrounded by recumbent figures and, in silhouette, the curved, serpentine prow of an Albine boat.

After silently beaching their craft a little way from the camp, they deployed in a semicircle, then charged. To their infinite surprise they met no resistance. The twenty sleeping men on the ground about the fire did not move a muscle.

Oro comprehended the situation at a glance. "Too much kova."

"But the girls," asked Grandon, "where are they? And where is Tholto?"

His question was partly answered by the sudden appearance of Rotha from the entrance of a nearby cave. With a smothered cry of thanksgiving she flung herself into the strong arms of Oro, who swung her off her feet in his exuberance of joy.

"Where is Vernia?" asked Grandon. "Tell me quickly — is she safe?"

Rotha hesitated as if fearful that he would strike her for her answer. "She is in that cave — with Tholto."

The cave she indicated was a short distance from the one she had just vacated. Grandon swung his spiked club free and, snatching a blazing brand from the fire, entered, followed by Oro and several others.

A solitary figure sat cross-legged in the middle of the floor. It was Tholto. He waited their coming with bowed head.

"What have you done with her, false friend?" demanded Grandon.

Tholto removed his helmet and cast it to the floor.

"Kill me, Grandon of Terra," he said sadly, in a tone totally unlike that of Tholto the braggart. "I bare my head to a just executioner. I am not fit to live."

"Answer my question, accursed slave. Where is our Torrogina?"

"I do not know. I left her here for a short time while I went for a drink or two of wine. When I returned she was gone. My head was reeling from the drink when I entered. Many years have passed since I tasted liquor and I overestimated my capacity. I sank to the floor and dreamed a horrible dream in which I saw her torn to pieces by a huge animal. She is dead — dead, and I am the cause."

"The fool is drunk," said Oro. "Pay no attention to his ravings. She is probably concealed somewhere nearby."

After binding Tholto and setting a man to guard him, they searched the cave, calling loudly for Vernia, but there was no reply. Rotha was positive that she had not left the cave previous to Tholto's entrance, as the mouth was only a few steps from the place where she had served drinks to the men, and she could not have missed seeing her.

Grandon's attention was attracted by a yawning hole about three feet in diameter, which had previously escaped his observation, as it was partly concealed by a section of jutting rock. He substituted a torch for the nearly consumed fire brand and entered on hands and knees followed by Oro. The opening grew large as they progressed, until they could stand erect.

Presently they emerged in the open air. They were in a fern forest, not more than a hundred feet from the camp, having come completely through the hill that screened it from the coast.

Oro stooped and, with a muttered exclamation, picked up some strips which had been torn from a sack and knotted together.

"She came this way," he said excitedly, "for here are the strips with which Tholto bound her."

"The dream of Tholto," he said, brokenly. "It is a reality. Look!"

On the ground before them was a pool of freshly congealed blood. Beside it lay a small Albine gauntlet — the gauntlet of Vernia!

As Grandon sorrowfully retraced his steps followed by the horrified Oro, he pressed the little Albine gauntlet to his lips. With a dazed feeling of unreality he sat down before the fire. All night long he sat there, staring at the licking flames, unmindful of what went on around him.

Tholto and his stupefied companions, disarmed and bound by Grandon's men, lay in a long row under the watchful eyes of four guards. The others slept, with the exception of Oro, who sat across the fire with Rotha, replenishing it from time to time. The two conversed in awed whispers, speculating on the possible fate of the culprits.

The dawn found Grandon gazing at a heap of smoking embers. His four weary guards wakened their slumbering companions and lay down for a well-earned rest. The stupefied drinkers slept on, oblivious of the sounds that went on about them, as the awakened men prepared the simple breakfast of hot roots and stewed mushrooms.

Marsh-men are expert fishermen, and four of them rigged some crude but efficient tackle by tearing up several food sacks for line, using thorns for hooks and stones for sinkers. They fished along the shore only a few yards from the camp and soon had caught more than the entire company could possibly eat. The fish were boiled in the same manner as the roots and mushrooms, and made a most pleasing addition to the morning meal.

When all was ready, Oro fearfully approached his young commander with a shell of steaming roots, another of mushrooms, and a toothsome fish. Mechanically, Grandon took the food and tried to eat, but it seemed that every morsel choked him. He rose unsteadily to his feet, as his legs were cramped and numb.

Grandon walked straight to where Tholto lay, bound and helpless. He called two of his men. "Remove his armor," he said curtly.

The command was obeyed with celerity, while the soldiers crowded around to see how the culprit was to be punished. When his armor was removed the prisoner stood silently, almost impassively, waiting his death sentence.

"I should kill you, Tholto," said Grandon, "yet I cannot bring myself to slay a helpless prisoner. You have proved yourself a man without a sense of honor or gratitude. As such, you are not fit to wear the armor or bear the weapons of a soldier of Granterra. I found you a naked, primitive savage, and return you thus to your native jungle. You will have a fighting chance for life. It is a slender one, but must be preferable to immediate death from your point of view. Go!"

Tholto, no less amazed than those about him at this unexpected reprieve, climbed the rugged hillside and disappeared over the brow.

Meanwhile, most of the sleeping deserters had awakened. They looked about them in astonishment, and several tried unsuccessfully to rise, but the bonds held them.

"Are we to let them go, also?" asked Oro.

"Cut their bonds, and see that all are thoroughly awakened."

The men were forthwith released, and the more drowsy were shaken until completely awake, after which they all stood before him, the deserters unarmed, surrounded by the others.

"I extend complete amnesty to you who forsook your country in its hour of need, following the leadership of Tholto, on one condition. That is, that you promise to return at once to Granterra, tell Joto all that has happened, and enlist your services with those who are fighting for supremacy of man in the Valley of the Sabits. Do you promise?"

To a man they assented eagerly.

"Give them their weapons and provisions," ordered Grandon. "Let them begin their journey now."

The craft was quickly loaded and pushed out to sea. When it had departed Grandon called his men around him once more.

"The quest that we began with some scant hope of success has ended in complete failure," he said sadly. "Last night when I learned of the death of our beloved princess I was ready and willing to die. One thought alone restrained me. I have a duty to perform. Far to the north of us live a people who have been enslaved and driven from their homes without cause. They made me prince of their country which they call Uxpo, and I fought in their behalf until Providence intervened. I cannot command you to accompany me on the journey I will begin today. Nor will I entreat you. If there be those among you who love adventure for its own sake, I extend the invitation to come with me and share the fortunes, or mayhap, the misfortunes of war. I make no promises, nor do I offer any rewards, though if Uxpo should win to freedom those who assisted in her deliverance will not go unremembered."

Oro was the first to speak. "Where Grandon of Terra leads, Oro follows," he said warmly.

"He fought for the freedom of our country," said another, "I am at your service, Grandon of Terra."

"And I — and I . . ." shouted the others in a chorus. "Lead us to Uxpo."

"Load the boat and make ready to push off," said Grandon. "We will start at once. Some three or four days' journey from here a great river empties into the Azpok. By following it we will come to Uxpo."

CHAPTER XVI

Prince Destho, now provisional emperor of Reabon, moved his slender, leonine form to a more comfortable position on the scarlet cushions of his throne and turned his countenance.

"Do you expect me to belied such a wild tale as this knave?" he growled. "Authentic reports had it that she and her four guards were devoured by a reptile nearly a year ago."

"I swear by the sacred bones of Thorth that it is she and none other. Having seen her daily at the Imperial Court of Reabon, how could I forget her?"

"Granted that the woman you found resembles the Princess of Reabon, how could it be possible that if lost in the mountains of Uxpo she would be discovered wandering on the edge of the great salt marsh along the Azpok Ocean?"

"I can only recount the facts, your majesty, and let your own eyes bear me witness when you see her. We were just preparing for our evening meal when this girl suddenly appeared from the mouth of a nearby cave. At sight of the men and torches she turned and attempted to escape, but tripped over a creeper and two of our men caught her before she could rise. As she was clad from head to foot in shining brown armor, I at first took her for a youth, but upon removing her helmet, discovered her identity, while concealing my own. After ordering the captain to bring her here unharmed, I hurried ahead to apprise your majesty of the good news."

"Do any of the men know who she is?"

"None recognized her, and I was careful not to betray her identity until I had learned your majesty's intentions."

"You have done well, Zueppa, and if she proves to be Vernia of Reabon you shall be highly rewarded. She must not, however, be brought here to the capital. The risk would be too great. Take her, instead, to my castle in my own kingdom, where every man is loyal to me, and where escape will be impossible. Matters of state delay me here, but I will be able to visit my castle in a few days. Take one of my swiftest motor vehicles and change the guard at the International Bridge before her arrival, posting only men from my own kingdom."

That evening, while Zueppa sipped his wine in the guard house at the international bridge, a small party of huntsmen arrived and presented their passports. With them were two prisoners, a beautiful girl in brown armor, and a huge, hairy marsh-man, whole sole article of attire was a loin cloth.

The young captain, after examining the passports of the hunts-men, looked at the prisoners. "And who are these?"

Vernia threw back her visor.

"The soldiers of Reabon do not question their rulers," she said.

The captain stared in open-mouthed amazement, then turned to a soldier who came up behind him.

"A striking resemblance to our princess," he muttered.

"She is an impostor," said the soldier. "Were we not warned of her coming?"

Vernia glared imperiously at the two men before her. "Have you forgotten the homage due your princess? Procure me a fast motor vehicle at once and have done with your insolence if you would see the light of another day."

Both men quickly bowed, with right hand extended, palm downward. Then a figure darted swiftly up behind them and kicked the bowing captain over on his face. In a flash Vernia recognized Zueppa.

"How now, idiots?" he shouted. "You were warned by our worthy sovereign, Destho, yet you make obeisance before this im-postor. Seize and bind her as you were ordered."

With a growl of fury, the hairy marsh-man leaped for the wily commander, but a score of soldiers rushed in and soon had him bound and helpless.

"Where did you get this brute, huntsmen?" asked Zueppa, looking at the still-struggling marsh-man.

"We captured him in the woods as he tried to steal our prisoner from us."

"Bring him to the castle of Prince Destho," he commanded. Then he lifted Vernia into his swift motor vehicle and sped away.

Some hours later the vehicle drew up before a massive gate. Zueppa answered the challenge of the guard and the lifting motors hummed sonorously. Vernia, half fainting, was taken from the ve-hicle and carried through a low arched doorway and along a dimly lighted corridor to a sparsely furnished suite of rooms where she was given over to the none-too-tender care of a tall, gaunt female slave.

The slave carefully locked the steel door and put the key in her belt pouch. For the first time in history, a ruler of Reabon was a pris-oner within the borders of the empire.

On the evening of the sixth day, Vernia lay face downward on her couch when footsteps sounded in the corridor. Her armor and hunting suit had been taken from her and replaced with the scarlet apparel of a princess. She sat up as a man entered — Prince Destho.

"Greetings, fair cousin," he said, placing a tray before her and locking the door. Destho had always been handsome in a flashy sort of way. Now as he stood in the gold and scarlet raiment of a rogi of Reabon, Vernia marveled at the change in his bearing.

"Your insolence is in keeping with your treason," she said.

"A thousand pardons if I have offended you, but I could not properly make obeisance in your presence, since our positions are reversed. Last year, you ruled supreme in Reabon; today I rule. I expect from you the deference due your sovereign."

"Expectation is far from realization," she replied.

"We shall see. There are ways of taming a proud spirit which may not have occurred to you — but pray do not force me to speak of them. I have come to offer you a pleasant and honorable way out of your difficulty."

"Which is . . . ?"

"It would have been easy to kill you, you know. My associates urged that course, but I sought more that that — to wed the most beautiful woman in all Zarovia." He raised his hand. "Hear me out, fair cousin; you cannot reverse history now. In ten days I will be Emperor of Reabon, while you are an expatriate. You know the laws that bind even the supreme ruler. The expatriate is an outcast, subject to seizure as a slave by the first free citizen who discovers him — or her. I would save you from that indignity."

"And what is this pleasant and honorable way out of the difficulty?"

"A marriage to your future emperor before the ten days are up. I will make you my empress, and together we will rule the mightiest empire in all Zarovia."

"So you would return the half of my birthright in exchange for my hand in marriage. It is a most magnanimous offer."

"It is far from being the worst I could make you. Where, on all Zarovia, could you find a man better suited to be your mate? My royal blood is on a par with yours. My bravery has been proved by the very coup that has placed you in my power. As for my looks, I assure you there are a thousand beautiful damsels who do not think me unhandsome and would jump at the offer I am making you."

"Your royal blood is an accident of birth, and your bravery is that of a man who seeks combat with those weaker than himself. I spurn your offer, traitor Destho. Pray, leave me now. Spare me the further insult of your insufferable presence."

Destho cleared the space between them and seized her roughly by the shoulders, forcing her back on the scarlet couch. "Take heed, lest the insult of my presence become a reality. I could . . ."

His words were cut short by the thunder of a heavy fist on the steel door. Furiously, he released the half-fainting girl and answered the summons, opening the door but a little way.

"How, now, Zueppa?" he demanded angrily. "What is the meaning of this intrusion? Did I not give you explicit orders not to disturb me for other than the most urgent business?"

"It is because of your highness's command that I have come. A messenger has just arrived with startling news of a revolt in the kingdom of Uxpo. He awaits your presence in the audience chamber."

"Another revolt in Uxpo? By the bones of Thorth! Will that kingdom never cease to trouble us?"

He turned to Vernia. "I regret that I must leave you thus hastily, fair cousin, but I will return presently to continue our interesting discussion."

He bowed sardonically from the doorway, then closed and locked the door after him. Vernia heard the retreating footsteps of the two men grow fainter in the corridor, finally dying away in the distance. She sank back on the couch.

She had heard the conversation of the two men, but, at first, placed no significance on the fact that there had been another revolution in Uxpo. Gradually, however, it came to her that there could be but one man with the ability to lead the Uxponians to a successful revolt — Grandon of Terra!

Some time later the gaunt slave woman came in to remove the dishes containing her untouched meal. Though she had always been sullenly taciturn in the past, Vernia resolved to question her.

"Have you heard aught of a revolt in Uxpo, Marsa?" she asked.

The sour features of the woman brightened perceptibly.

"It is the talk of the castle," she replied. "The capital has fallen into the hands of the Fighting Traveks and every Reabonian soldier has been killed, captured or driven from the kingdom."

"You seem elated at the news," said Vernia, noting the unusually cheerful demeanor of her custodian.

"And well I may be," she answered, "for I am of Uxpo. I was captured and brought here a slave by the armies of your father, Emperor Margo. These are the most glorious tidings I have heard in years."

"No doubt revolt was led by Bordeen, commander of the Fighting Traveks," said Vernia in as casual a manner as she could assume.

"By Bordeen, say you? Hardly, though no doubt he took a part in it. Prince Thaddor, who now calls himself Grandon of Terra, reappeared as suddenly and mysteriously as he disappeared nearly a year ago. It is said that he wears a suit of brown armor that will turn even a mattork projectile and carries weapons of the same strange metal, which cuts steel as easily as a scarbo's blade cuts wood. Report has it, also, that he brought with him a bodyguard of twenty men from a far country, similarly garbed and armed. And I understand that yesterday he was formally crowned King of Uxpo."

"Would you be willing, Marsa, to do a favor for Grandon of Terra, the savior of Uxpo, if the opportunity offered?"

"I would willingly risk my life for him, even as he has risked his for my beloved country," replied Marsa fervently.

"And would you be averse to performing the task if it favored me as well?"

The brow of Marsa clouded. "You have always been the most bitter enemy of Uxpo. My husband was slain by your father's soldiers and I was enslaved by them. You, in turn, twice led your armies into Uxpo for conquest and pillage. You ordered the execution of our valiant King Lugi and sent Prince Thaddor himself to wear his life away in the marble quarries. A favor to you could not possibly be a favor to the King of Uxpo."

She took up the tray and turned to go.

"One moment, Marsa," entreated Vernia. "There is reason and justice in what you say; nevertheless, I am sure I can convince you that you will favor Grandon of Terra by assisting me."

Marsa paused. At length she said: "I must go now, but I will return presently. There can be no harm in listening."

"Return as soon as possible," replied Vernia as the slave inserted the key in the lock, "or you may be too late."

The dreary minutes dragged into hours, and hope was fast falling when footsteps sounded in the corridor and a key rattled in the lock. Vernia rose and moved toward the door with hope renewed — then paused in alarm — for the doorway framed the burly figure of Zueppa. To her surprise, he bowed low with right hand extended palm downward, then paused respectfully, waiting for her to speak.

"What spirit of irony brings you to make mock-obeisance at this unseemly hour?" asked Vernia.

"I come not in irony, your majesty," replied Zueppa, "but in all humility to crave forgiveness for the great wrong I have done my sovereign, and to offer my services."

"You could not choose a more fitting time for such an offer — and if it be genuine, for full forgiveness and perhaps an additional reward, should it be merited."

Zueppa softly closed the door.

"I betray a secret that would forfeit my life if divulged in this castle, when I tell you that I am in sympathy with Uxpo. Though my father was a Reabonian noble, my mother was from Uxpo, and it was with her and with her country that my sympathies always lay. One in this castle who is loyal to Uxpo had enlisted me in your cause. When you were my country's most bitter enemy, I plotted your downfall. But Prince Destho has become even a worse enemy to Uxpo than you were, and now that the conditions are reversed I am willing to change my position for a loyal promise — the sole conditions to be, first, a proclamation freeing my countrymen, and second, a pardon for myself."

"I have already promised another to free Uxpo," replied Vernia, "and I willingly add to it the promise of complete and unconditional pardon for you if you can do one of two things — either arrange my escape to Reabon before my year is up, or immediately send a message to Grandon of Terra, in order that he may come to my rescue."

"I had already thought of the former plan," said Zueppa, "and made some preparations for it. I will leave now and send Marsa to you with clothing in which you will pass for a castle slave. When all is quiet I will return and conduct you through a secret passageway to a place outside the castle where I keep a swift motor vehicle. We will thus be able to reach the capital by morning."

"And Tholto, the marsh-man. I would have him released also."

"Tholto escaped from our guards as they were bringing him to the castle. No doubt he is back in his native haunts by now."

As he bowed low and departed, hope rose in the bosom of Vernia.

After Zueppa closed and carefully locked the door of her chamber, he made straight for the quarters of the salves, but his way was blocked by a castle guard before he had gone a dozen steps.

"Out of my way, fellow," he roared, expecting cringing obedience.

The soldier met his frown calmly. "His Highness, Prince Destho, commands your immediate presence in the audience chamber."

Zueppa turned, without a word, and followed the guard. "It is the end," he thought. "Our plot has been discovered." In spite of his misgiving, however, he proceeded serenely to the foot of the throne and made obeisance. To his surprise, Destho received him cordially, descending from the dais to take him by the hand.

"Come, let us walk in the garden, excellent Zueppa," he said. "I would confer with you about our plans for the recapture of Uxpo. The stuffy air of the castle fogs my brain."

"I should be happy to learn," said Zueppa, preceding Prince Destho into the garden, "that your highness favorably considers my admonition to abandon the reconquest of Uxpo until established firmly on the throne. Much can happen in a short time, and it is possible . . ."

His words ended in a gasp of pain. Moaning feebly, he slumped to the ground, as a dagger sank to the hilt in his back. Destho tore the weapon from the wound and calmly wiped it on the clothing of the prostrate man.

"Thus should all traitors die. I have been lenient with you, after all, for you are a double traitor; first to your princess, then to me."

He turned and entered the castle. On reaching the audience chamber he summoned the captain of the castle guards.

"Has Marsa been confined in the dungeon?" he asked.

"She has, your highness, with heavy manacles and the spiked collar about her neck as directed."

He dismissed the captain with a nod, then picked up a long, flexible tube, one end of which passed into the floor behind the throne. On the free end was a bell-shaped contrivance which he held to his ear. He listened intently for some time, then smiled grimly, as he head the sound of subdued sobbing.

The tube connected with a sound amplifier which was concealed behind a grating in the room where Vernia was imprisoned.

The plans of Prince Destho for the reconquest of Uxpo were materializing rapidly, as he breakfasted leisurely in the throne room of his castle several days later. He had sent no less than fifty hired assassins to slay Grandon, and, if this failed, had a huge army of thirty thousand men assembled in and around his stronghold, ready to march on the rebellious kingdom.

A courier, dusty and bedraggled, was hurried before the throne.

"How now, Torbo?" asked Destho, glancing down at the courier. "What tidings from Uxpo?"

"Grandon of Terra has been slain and his body lies in state at the royal palace!"

"Great news, if true. Who slew him?"

"I do not know, but it is rumored that the men who succeeded in the attempt were, themselves, slain."

"Did you see the body?"

"I did, your majesty, and the features were so horribly mutilated as to be unrecognizable. I also regret to inform your majesty that your chief assassin, Malcabar, was slain yesterday morning."

Destho turned to his councilors. "We will not disband our army yet," he said. "I must have a further confirmation of this."

A few minutes later, two of the castle guards entered, ushering between them a tall, bearded man in the uniform of a soldier of Reabon. All three made the customary salute before the throne, then they arose, and the two guards stepped back, leaving the tall soldier in the center of the floor.

"Whom have we here?" asked Destho, addressing one of the guards.

"His papers proclaim him one Xantol of Uxpo, resident helper of the spy, Malcabar, and a bearer of tidings for your highness."

Destho looked long and appraisingly at the soldier. It seemed that those black eyes were searching the usurper's very soul.

"Your tidings, Xantol," snapped Destho.

"I have been sent to inform your highness of a rumor being circulated in Uxpo, to the effect that Grandon of Terra has been slain."

"A rumor, say you? You bring us stale news, fellow. We have already been apprised that the villainous imposter is dead and that his mutilated body lies in state in the palace."

Destho turned to the guard. "Who signed this man's papers?"

"They are signed by Malcabar."

"By Malcabar? Let me see them."

He examined the papers carefully. "The writing and signature seem genuine," he said. "Send the courier in again!"

As Torbo re-entered, bowing low, Destho snarled. "So! You found it expedient to lie to me, Torbo!"

"I — lie to your highness?" exclaimed Torbo in surprise. "Surely it pleases your highness to jest with his humble servant."

"You told me Malcabar was slain yesterday morning. I have here a letter, written and signed by him last evening. Can the dead write letters?"

"If you have a letter from Malcabar, then indeed can the dead write letters, for I swear by the bones of Thorth that I saw him lead the attack on the usurper yesterday morning and a huge armored guard clove him from crown to chin."

Destho looked searchingly from Torbo to the soldier, and from the soldier back to Torbo.

"One of you lies, that is certain," he said, "and you may rest assured, both of you, that the guilty man will be discovered and dealt with for his perfidy."

"May I ask who brought the letter?" asked Torbo.

"I brought the letter," replied the soldier.

"And who are you?"

"Xantol of Uxpo, resident helper of Malcabar."

Torbo flushed angrily. "This man lies," he said. "Malcabar had no Uxponian helpers. All were men of Reabon, and all died with him yesterday morning."

"You were acquainted with Malcabar's assistants?" asked Destho.

"Every one of them."

"And you have never seen this man before?"

"I have seen him somewhere," replied Torbo, knitting his brows. "His face is familiar yet unfamiliar." He approached the soldier and scanned his features carefully. Then he burst into a loud laugh.

"Shoot me for a hahoe if this man wears not a false beard," he said, and to prove his statement he suddenly reached forward and plucked a handful of hair from the man's face.

The Uxponian whipped out his scarbo, but strong arms pinioned his own from behind, and, in a moment, he was deprived of his blade and stood helpless in the grip of the two burly guards.

"Pluck a few more feathers from this bird and see if you can identify him," said Destho.

"This is unnecessary," replied Torbo, "for I have recognized him already. He is Grandon of Terra!"

Had a thunderbolt crashed through the arched ceiling at that moment it could hardly have created more surprise. Destho was dumbfounded.

"Grandon of Terra?" he exclaimed. "But you told me that he was dead."

"I did not tell you that I saw him die," replied Torbo, "and this man here is unquestionably Grandon of Terra."

A gleam of triumph shone in the eyes of Destho at these words.

"You are more a fool than I took you to be, Grandon of Terra," he said. "Perhaps even more of a fool than you took me for."

"It is possible that I surpass you in folly. You have, however, two more qualities on which I must yield you all honors."

"And those are . . ."

"Treachery and cowardice!"

"Away with him," Destho said. "Let him meditate on his folly in the darkness of the dungeon until we have use for him."

The burly guards hustled Grandon out of a side door and along a narrow passage to a winding stairway which seemed to lead into the very bowels of the planet, so long were they in descending. After manacling his wrists and ankles they pushed him into a dark, foul-smelling hole and slammed and fastened a heavy metal door which fitted so snugly that not the tiniest ray of light was admitted.

As he lay on the damp, slimy floor, Grandon pondered the words of Destho. The phrase "until we have use for him" was puzzling. After a short interval, two guards entered Grandon's dungeon, removed the manacles from his ankles, and led him up the spiral stairway.

They did not go all the way to the top, but turned off through a narrow doorway which Grandon judged to be about halfway to the ground level. A short walk along a dimly-lighted passage brought them to an underground chamber which looked to Grandon like a workshop or laboratory of some sort, for it contained several unusual appearing contrivances.

In one corner was a raised circular platform covered with a resilient material greatly resembling rubber. He noticed that there was a hole in the center of the platform, and that a pipe, evidently connected with the hole, led from under it to a small motor which stood nearby. A huge glass bell was suspended by a pulley above the platform and a steel chair stood beside it. The only other articles of furniture in the room were a wooden chair and table on which were writing materials.

The two guards chained Grandon to the steel chair and, lifting him between them, placed him on the raised platform directly above the hole.

A moment later Destho entered. He looked at Grandon with a grim smile. Then he turned to the nearest guard.

"I see you have things in readiness. Now bring her imperial majesty and see that her face be veiled so that none may recognize her on the way."

Scarce had the guard left to do the bidding of his master ere Bopo, captain of Destho's private guards, entered. "Where is the document, dolt?" demanded Destho. "Have you failed to prepare it?"

"Here," replied Bopo, drawing a scroll from beneath his garments. "I kept it hid, as your majesty commanded secrecy in the matter."

"Good. Let me have it."

Destho read the document hastily. Then he read it again more slowly.

"Are you sure this is the correct legal form?"

"I am positive, your majesty."

Destho placed the scroll on the table, then crossed the room and bowed politely as the guard returned, leading a woman whose face was heavily veiled.

Suddenly she flung back her veil and rushed forward with a little smothered cry, paying no attention whatever to Destho. Grandon's heart leaped to his throat at sight of her pale face and golden tresses.

"Vernia!" He would have risen, but the chains held him.

"My Grandon — my hero!" she cried as her lips found his and clung there, and her arms went around his neck. He tried to lift his manacled hands to smooth her hair as she buried her face on his shoulder, sobbing incoherently.

"But why did you come here alone — to certain death?"

Grandon whispered his answer in her ear. "Zueppa, though fearfully wounded, managed to reach me with tidings of your whereabouts. It would have been futile to bring my small army, so I came alone, disguised as the helper of an assassin who attempted my life!"

"Enough of this whispering!" said Destho, smiling as he tore her from her lover and led her to the chair beside the table.

"A pleasant surprise I prepared for you, fair cousin, was it not?" Destho said. "You have had your little emotional outburst. Now let us get down to business. I have a document here which needs only your signature to make it legal. Read it aloud, Bopo, that all may hear and bear witness."

Bopo took the scroll and advanced pompously to the center of the floor. He unrolled it with a flourish, cleared his throat, and read:

"'A Proclamation by Her Imperial Majesty, Vernia, Princess of Reabon:

"'On the twenty-fourth day of the eighth Endir in the four thousand and tenth year of Thorth, I, Vernia of Reabon, hereby proclaim and declare to all my subjects throughout the length and breadth of the empire that I have taken for my husband, and raised to the office of emperor, to rule over me and my people, the brave and illustrious Prince Destho.

"'It is my command that copies of this proclamation be made and distributed to all parts of the empire without delay, and that the fifth day of the ninth Endir be set aside as a day for feasting and suitable celebration in honor of this momentous event.'"

He finished and handed the scroll to Destho, who spread it on the table before Vernia.

She looked up with flashing eyes. "Surely you do not expect me to sign such a ridiculous document?"

"You refuse?"

For answer she seized it and flung it from her.

"More temperament," said Destho, coolly, picking up the scroll. "You compel me to use persuasion."

He made a sign to the guard, who grinned broadly and, loosing the chain by which the glass bell was suspended, lowered it until it rested firmly on the elastic edges of the platform where Grandon sat, calm and immobile in the iron chair.

"It is plainly evident," said Destho, "that you have some regard for yonder doomed man."

Vernia started at his words.

"Though he is a rebel and traitor, you could have saved his life, merely by signing your name. As it is, you shall have the pleasure of witnessing his death struggles. Start the motor."

The burly guard crossed to the motor with a grin more broad than before, and pressed a button.

Vernia, peering intently through the glass, saw Grandon flinch slightly when the thing started. Then he compressed his lips and settled back as if resolved to meet his fate calmly. Presently he noticed that he was breathing convulsively with nostrils distended.

"Stop! You are killing him!" she screamed. "Stop that terrible thing. I will sign. I will do anything."

Destho made a sign to the guard, who pressed another button and opened a valve, but not before Grandon's head had sunk limply forward. There was a loud hissing sound and he raised his head, gasping weakly.

"I thought you might be brought to reason, stubborn and head-strong as you are," said Destho with a smile of triumph.

He placed the scroll before her and she paused for a moment, for Grandon was looking at her through the glass and shaking his head emphatically. "I cannot do it," she said weakly.

"Very well," replied Destho. He turned to the guard. "Start the motor. There will be no stopping it this time."

"No, no!" cried Vernia. "Do not start it. I will sign."

Again Destho motioned for the guard to desist. Vernia held the scroll, half rolled before her. She looked at Grandon for a moment as if in silent farewell. Then she tore her eyes from his with a visible effort and resolutely affixed her name to the document.

Destho seized it eagerly and examined the signature. Then he rolled it up, stuffed it in his bosom, walked to the motor, closed the valve and pressed the button.

Vernia, sensing his purpose, screamed frantically and ran to shut the thing off, but he intercepted her and forced her back in the chair.

"I am legal emperor of Reabon now," he said. "There is no more need for force, for my word is law. I now decree that this traitor shall die, and you, in company with your beloved husband, will have the pleasure of watching his death struggles."

CHAPTER XVII

When the glass bell was lowered around him Grandon rightly guessed that the thing was intended either to torture or kill him — perhaps both.

He gritted his teeth, though he flinched when the guard started the motor. A roaring sounded in his ears. Were they pumping some sort of deadly gas into the bell? He could detect no unusual odor of any kind. Breathing, however, was rapidly growing more and more difficult.

It was then he guessed the truth. They were pumping the air out of the bell! Fearful pains shot through his body as he gasped and struggled for breath. Suddenly all went black before him and his ead drooped forward.

A moment later, apparently, he was revived by the sibilant inrush of air. He saw Vernia, apparently ready to sign the proclamation which would make her the lawful wife of Destho, and shook his head vigorously.

Though he could not hear what was said, he saw her refusal, the subsequent threat of Destho, and her final acquiescence.

"Don't sign!" he shouted, but she was looking away from him and his voice did not reach beyond the thick wall of glass.

It was this and final treachery of Destho in again starting the motor that filled him with a consuming rage and aroused him from his passivity. With a burst of strength of which he had not known himself capable, he strained at his shackles. A chain parted — then another. His arms were free. He reached down and wrenched at the fetters which held his legs. Again the roaring sounded in his ears. A quick jerk freed his right leg. He twisted the chair from his left and swung it against the glass with all his might. A thousand tiny cracks radiated from the point where it struck. He swung again. There was a crash and a hollow report like the crack of a tork as the air surged inwards.

The guard stood ready to receive him with drawn scarbo as Grandon leaped out. Swinging the iron chair, he crushed the man's skull like an eggshell, and his scarbo clattered to the floor. The other guard, rushing to the assistance of his companion, met a similar fate.

Destho was dragging Vernia from the room. Bopo still faced Grandon, scarbo in hand. He hurled the chair, which caught the surprised captain amidships. Grandon picked up the scimitar-bladed scarbo of the guard and ran forward to intercept Destho.

With Grandon's blade threatening him, the usurper was forced to release Vernia and draw his weapon. The man was no mean swordsman and, for a time, the outcome was uncertain.

The Earthman fought in a blind fury. Gradually, his brain cleared and his stroke became more certain. He forced his antagonist to the wall and, with a dexterous twist, sent his scarbo clattering.

A look of alarm shone in the eyes of the amazed Rebonian price. "Would you kill an unarmed man?"

"Surrender or . . ."

Before Grandon could finish the sentence the wily Destho dodged under his arm and ran through the door, calling loudly for help.

Grandon started after him — the paused hopelessly.

"Come," he said, taking Vernia's hand. "He will have a swarm of soldiers here in a few moments. We must try to find a hiding place."

They sped down the dim passageway, hand in hand. Ahead of them they heard footsteps and the clank of arms. A doorway on their left offered temporary haven, and into this they darted. Grandon held the door slightly ajar and watched. In a moment a dozen of the castle guards rushed past, followed by Destho.

"Now," he whispered. "We must go quietly."

Again they darted along the passageway until they arrived at the spiral stair. They had barely ascended to the ground level when a guard appeared. Grandon ran him through the throat, but not before he let out a shriek that brought a score of his comrades running.

There was nothing for it but to climb the stairway, and this they did, only to be spied by the foremost guard. He dashed after them, calling his companions to follow, and paid for his temerity with a split skull when he came up with them at the fourth level. His comrades, finding his body a moment later, set up an angry shout and redoubled their speed.

Before they reached the seventh level, Grandon was forced to turn and engage the foremost guard. The man proved a poor swordsman, and a quick thrust through the heart sent him back to his fellows, momentarily impeding their progress.

Taking advantage of this opportunity, Grandon turned and again fled up the stairs with Vernia. They passed the eighth level before noticing that they were in a narrow tower overlooking the sloping roof. The tenth level was the last, and Grandon thrust Vernia into the tower room before turning to face their pursuers.

They were fairly trapped.

The first foeman, a huge coarse-featured giant, felt the weight of Grandon's steel and toppled back with a groan. Another leaped over his body and took his place, only to go down before the bewildering swordplay of the Earthman. Then they tried rushing him two at a time, but as two men could not wield their scarbos simultaneously in the narrow passage, they quickly shared the fate of the others.

When they could no longer mount over their fallen comrades, they withdrew a little way and Grandon judged from the murmur of their voices that they were formulating another plan of attack. He took advantage of the lull in the fighting to strip a tork and belt from the nearest man. Then he lay down at the head of the stair with tork leveled and waited.

Suddenly he heard a familiar whining sound, followed by a terrific explosion that shook the floor. A mattork projectile! Could it be that they were shelling the tower? There followed another and another in quick succession — then a continuous roar, as though a hundred mattork cannon had gone into action.

Vernia called excitedly from the tower room.

"An army approaches through the forest. I can see their uniforms through the trees and they look like Fighting Traveks. Ah, they *are* Fighting Traveks! A company of them is charging through the camp while their mattorks shell the castle. A small band of men in Albine armor fight with them in the front ranks. Destho's troops were momentarily thrown into confusion, but now they are rallying! Oh, they will kill all the Traveks, for they outnumber them ten to one."

"Can you see who leads the Traveks?" asked Grandon, not daring to leave his post.

"He is a big man with a gray beard. He towers above his men, urging them on to battle with a voice that roars deep and strong!"

"Bordeen!" exclaimed Grandon. So the doughty commander had disobeyed orders. Evidently Oro and his twenty marsh-men fought with them.

"The army of Destho has rallied," continued Vernia. "They are closing in on the Traveks from two sides. They are butchering them — it is terrible. Now the Traveks are retreating. They are cutting their way back to their comrades, but already half of their number has fallen. Now a new company charges to their rescue while the mattorks sweep the lines on both sides of them. The survivors have succeeded in reaching their comrades, but the army of Destho is surrounding them."

"The fools — the utter fools," moaned Grandon.

Again Vernia cried out in amazement.

"A new army approaches from the south. The camp is deserted on that side, all having gone to surround the Traveks on the north. A host of warriors in Albine armor is charging across the clearing. The army of Destho is rushing back to engage them and the men on the walls shower bullets on them without effect. They have clashed with Destho's men and cut them down like reeds. Not a single warrior in brown armor has fallen. Now the men on the wall are training mattorks on them. The mattork projectiles tear great holes in their ranks, yet they forge steadily ahead. I can see their banners now. They are inscribed with the word 'Granterra!'"

"It must be Joto," said Grandon. "Yet how could he have learned of our presence here?"

"It is Joto," cried Vernia, joyously. "He is fighting in the front ranks with his visor raised, cheering his men between blows and laughing as he fights."

"There is not another leader like him."

"Now the Traveks have rallied. They are shelling the batteries on the walls. They are cutting their way through the army of Destho."

"Would that I could help them!" cried Grandon.

"More warriors in brown armor are approaching," continued Vernia. "They are accompanied by an army of sabits. The men have mounted on the backs of the sabits and are charging the castle. The sabits are carrying them up and over the walls which they could not have scaled unaided. They are swarming everywhere. The sabits crush the defenders in their forceps and the mounted men cut them down with their swords. Now the walls and the courtyard have been cleared of defenders! The gate has been thrown open and they are storming the castle itself, the Traveks fighting side by side with the armored warriors."

Grandon was so engrossed in Vernia's description of the battle that he momentarily relaxed his vigil. He nearly paid for his carelessness with his life, for a tork bullet sang uncomfortably close to his ear, and a new company of guardsmen charged up the stairs. As he quickly returned the fire he heard a voice — the voice of Destho — on the level below. "Remember. Ten thousand acres of choice land to the man who slays him, but harm not the woman."

"Go back, fools," shouted Grandon. "Dead men have no use for land."

But neither his threat nor his bullets could stay them. The men who surged up the steps fired their torks as they came and carried long-bladed spears. He was compelled to retreat to the tower room where he found momentary safety by barring the steel door.

There was a shout of baffled rage, and a rain of blows sounded on the door. "It will hold them off for awhile — a very short while, I fear."

He was startled by a scream from Vernia. Turning, he beheld the ugly head of a red-mouthed sabit, peering in at the window. Behind it appeared the spiny crest of an Albine-armored warrior. Both squeezed through the narrow window and the warrior threw back his visor.

"Tholto!" exclaimed Grandon and Vernia simultaneously.

Leaping from his savage mount, the marsh-man prostrated himself before them, right hand extended palm downward.

"Tholto, your slave," he said simply.

Grandon, noting that the steel door was sagging from the terrific blows of those without, leaped forward with scarbo ready. Tholto followed, baring his sword, and, as he did so, speaking a few words to the sabit in the tone language. The creature responded by vibrating its antennae and took a place between them, directly in front of the door, where it waited expectantly with its head cocked to one side, much as a terrier waits for the leap of a cornered rat.

The door fell inward with a rending crash and a shout of triumph went up from the attackers. Then the sabit leaped, snapping to the right and left with its powerful forceps and shearing a man in twain with each snap. With Grandon swinging his scarbo on one side and Tholto his sharp Albine sword on the other, the landing was cleared in a twinkling.

The bloodthirsty sabit plowed down the stairway, and the death shrieks of the fleeing guards were terrible to hear as it caught up with them one by one.

Grandon searched for Destho among the corpses that littered the landing, but he was not among them. Evidently he had escaped or was numbered among the sabit's victims, whose shrieks still sounded from below at intermittent intervals.

A ringing cheer floated up from the courtyard, and Grandon looked down from the tower window. Far below him he saw a straggling line of Destho's soldiers filing out from the castle, weaponless, and with their hands held out before them in token of submission. A detachment of Traveks escorted them on one side, while a company of the brown-armored soldiers of Granterra marched on the other.

"The castle has fallen," said Grandon. "Let us descend."

They picked their way down the blood-soaked steps while

Tholto ran ahead, calling his ferocious steed in the tone language of the sabits. The mangled bodies that strewed the entire stairway mutely attested the terrible efficiency of the fighting monster.

Upon reaching the ground level they made their way toward the audience chamber, whence came the unmistakable sounds of heated argument.

Shouts of "Kill the traitor!" and "Behead the assassin!" were distinguishable above the clamor.

"Oh, what are they doing?" cried Vernia. "Let us hurry."

When they entered the audience chamber they found it jammed with a crowd of Fighting Traveks and Granterrites, mingled indiscriminately. As they waved their swords and scarbos aloft, Destho, the object of their hatred, stood trembling with fright before the throne in the grip of two brawny Traveks. Bordeen, on one side, and Joto on the other, were attempting to quiet the angry mob.

"Wait, fools," roared Bordeen. "He has not told us where we may find Grandon of Terra and the princess. A dead man discloses no secrets."

"Torture him!" cried a brawny Travek.

"The secret is out," said Joto, "for Grandon of Terra approaches, and with him is the princess!"

At sight of Grandon and his fair companion the assembled fighting men sent up a shout that dwarfed their previous clamor to insignificance. A path was speedily cleared for the pair as they made their way toward the throne. Bordeen and Joto rushed forward to greet them, followed by Oro, Rotha and Tholto.

"I thought the hahoe of Reabon had killed you," said Bordeen huskily, tears of joy gleaming in his eyes. "We searched every dungeon and cell without a trace."

"A hahoe slays not a warrior so easily," said Joto, smiling broadly.

"The warrior was fairly cornered by the hahoes when you came so gallantly to the rescue," said Grandon. "How did you learn of our plight and how could you bring such a large army here without imperiling your people? The sabits may attack them during your absence."

"It was Tholto told us of the plight of the princess," said Joto. "We did not know that you had come here on the same mission as our own until informed by the Traveks. Tholto traveled unarmed and alone through the forests and the great salt marsh. There he built himself a crude raft with which he navigated the underground river. I came near beheading him before he convinced me that he was telling the truth. As for the safety of our people, there is no more danger in the Valley of the Sabits. Every sabit community has been subjected and man rules supreme. We lead indolent lives in Granterra, for our sabit slaves work for us, hunt for us and even fight for us. My only fear is that we may degenerate through inactivity."

"And you," said Grandon, turning to Bordeen. "How came you to disobey orders?"

"As soon as you had gone," Bordeen said, "I thought of the odds against you and realized that your quest was hopeless. I called all the captains in council and explained the situation. To a man they voted to come to your rescue. We felt that, though we might not be able to reach you, we might at least disconcert those within the castle sufficiently to give you an opportunity to escape."

"You did nobly," said Grandon, "yet my heart bleeds for the gallant soldiers who have sacrificed their lives today."

There was a sudden outcry from the direction of the throne. The wily Destho, taking advantage of the fact that all eyes were riveted on Grandon and Vernia, had broken from his guards and bolted for the door.

A dozen soldiers ran to intercept him, but to no purpose. He ran down the hallway and disappeared from view around a corner.

Grandon, Bordeen and Tholto, in hot pursuit, were only a few seconds behind him, yet when they turned the corner no one was in sight. The hall was lined with doorways, and Grandon plunged into one while his comrades entered the others. He found him himself in an empty room, lighted by a small window which stood open. Suddenly he heard the roar of a motor vehicle in the yard outside and ran to the window. He shouted a warning to the soldiers out side, but too late. The vehicle, gathering momentum with every revolution of its huge single wheel, shot through the gate and down the road before the astonished soldiers realized what it was all about. They sent a volley of tork bullets and curses after it as it disappeared around a curve in the road.

Calling his comrades, Grandon returned to where Vernia awaited them in the throne room. "We must hurry to Reabon at once," he said. "Destho has escaped."

"Did he take the proclamation with him?" asked Vernia.

Bordeen spoke up. "He could not have taken the proclamation with him, because we deprived him of all papers in his possession when he was made prisoner. I have them with me now."

He produced a bundle of papers which Grandon scanned eagerly. They were all letters from his spies and fellow conspirators. The proclamation was not among them.

"Your searchers must have overlooked it," said Grandon, "for it is not among these papers."

"That is possible, of course, but not probable," replied Bordeen. "He was searched thoroughly."

"Perhaps he disposed of it in some other way," suggested Joto.

"We may be able to find out from some of his officers, if any of them have been captured alive," said Grandon.

"Most of those left in the castle surrendered," Bordeen said. "Let us see what they have to say."

A dozen of them were produced forthwith and questioned. All declared that Destho had dispatched a messenger to the capital in a swift motor vehicle shortly before the attack by the Traveks. It was understood that the messenger was conveying an important document to Bonal, Prime Minister of Reabon.

"Copies will have been made and distributed and broadcast through the empire by this time," said Bordeen. "What was the nature of the proclamation? No doubt it favored Destho in some way or he would not have rushed it to the capital."

Grandon ground his teeth. "It favored Destho, all right, for it made him Emperor of Reabon and the husband of Vernia."

Joto laid his arm across Grandon's shoulders.

"My friend," he said gravely, "be not so downcast, I beg of you. Your enemy had the proclamation, but you still have Vernia of Reabon, and an army that is all but invincible. Let us march to Reabon at once."

Grandon turned to Vernia. "With your permission."

A smile overspread her face as she calmly replied: "I will go with you. Let us start at once."

CHAPTER XVIII

It was a picturesque procession that started for Reabon shortly after midnight. Destho's two-score motor vehicles and a number of carts had been pressed into use. All were equipped with bright searchlights, fore and aft, that lighted the road and reflected brilliantly from the armor and weapons of the marching men.

Grandon rode in the lead with Bordeen and Joto, commanders of the two armies whose victory had turned to defeat by the laws of the empire. Princess Vernia and Rotha followed in the car immediately behind them.

The Earthman rode in moody silence, nor did his two companions interrupt his thoughts. As the motors were throttled down to conform to the speed of the marching men, their progress was quite slow. Morning found them a good half day's march from the capital.

Grandon was startled by a sudden cry from the driver. At the same time their vehicle came to a full stop, and shouts of wonder and alarm echoed from without. He drew his scarbo, and leaped from the car. To his surprise he beheld a huge ball, more than fifty feet in diameter, blocking the road. Many of the soldiers, as well as occupants of the other cars, were running toward it.

"What is that thing?" he asked a young Travek.

"I do not know, your majesty," the man replied. "They who first saw it say it fell from the sky."

Grandon approached the globe and examined it curiously. It appeared to be constructed of a metal similar to asbestos, crisscrossed with a network of wires. Near the center of the side he faced was a circle of metal that suggested aluminum. The circle began to turn, and a murmur of surprise went up from the watchers.

Grandson's first thought was that a spaceship from Earth had reached Venus — but an instant's reflection made him reject this solution. Earth was probably not even a habitable planet now, and might not become so for millennia to come. Could this be from Mars, which also had a scientific culture now?

The circle was revolving more quickly now, and projecting from the sphere. Vernia came up beside the Earthman, Rotha following her. "What is it?"

"I don't know. It may be some new implement of war. You had best go back into the car until we find out." She complied quite meekly, he thought, as he turned to the soldiers and ordered them to stand back a hundred yards or so.

Now a screw-like cylinder projected from the globe for more than five feet. He could plainly see the threaded sides as it hung there, twenty-five feet above his head. It fell forward with a loud click and hung suspended by a thick hinge, disclosing a dark hole. From this hole, a ladder of flexible material dropped, one end nearly touching the ground.

Now the figure of a man in a spacesuit clearly similar to American design appeared and clambered down the ladder. He stood there a moment, looking at Grandon, then removed his helmet, and the Earthman recognized the features of Dr. Morgan.

"How are you, my boy?" he asked cordially.

Grandon snapped his fingers and grinned back. "You built another space-time vehicle, I see, Doctor — or did Vorn Vangal do it?"

Morgan smiled. "I wondered if you would remember. This is Vorn Vangal's work, operated by telekinesis like the Olban airship. Watch."

Even as he spoke, the huge globe moved upward from its resting place and hovered a hundred feet above their heads. "Suppose we climb into this vehicle of yours and I'll tell you the news while we ride to Reabon."

Grandon's reply was interrupted by a cry from several of the men and saw they were looking to the westward; he turned to behold a huge fleet of Olban airships bearing down on them. The ships were many times larger than the Olban craft he'd seen, but were constructed on the same general principles. Each airship had ten shining glass cabs and bristled with mattorks, projecting fore and aft, on both sides and below.

The fleet came to a dead stop above them. Then one airship descended to the spot where the globe of Dr. Morgan had rested a moment before, and a set of aluminum stairs which had been telescoped on the deck was elongated and flung over the side, reaching the ground.

Two men descended. The foremost was clad in scarlet apparel, trimmed with gold and glittering with precious jewels. His feet were incased in sandals of the softest frella hide, and he wore a turban-like headpiece, also an enormous glittering ruby that blazed from the middle of his forehead. His companion was more soberly garbed in purple trimmed with silver and also ornamented with jewels.

Grandon recognized the handsome, smooth-shaven youth in scarlet as "Harry Thorne" — actually the Martian, Borgen Takkor, who had followed him to Venus. The man in purple was Vorn

Vangal. At the same moment Thorne saw the doctor and ran forward, embracing him with a glad cry of recognition. He greeted Grandon with a warm handclasp.

It was not necessary to introduce Dr. Morgan and Vorn Vangal.

"Where is this beautiful princess of yours, Grandon?" asked Dr. Morgan. "I am anxious to meet her."

"And I also," supplemented Thorne, "though there is a certain princess back in Olba whose beauty I have not seen matched on three planets."

"I think," smiled Vorn Vangal, "you will find that opinions are quite likely to vary on such things as the beauty of a woman."

Grandon could not find the heart to reply.

"What ails you, man?" asked Thorne. "You look as if Vangal here has pronounced sentence of death on you."

"Buck up, my boy," said Dr. Morgan. "You haven't lost her yet."

"Haven't lost her? Didn't she sign a marriage decree making Destho her husband and Emperor of Reabon?"

He led them to Vernia's vehicle. She received them graciously, with all the dignity and poise of a born princess.

"And now," said the doctor when the presentation was concluded, "where are Bordeen and Joto?"

"What do you know about Bordeen and Joto?" asked Grandon in surprise.

"You forget that I have been in telepathic *rapport* with you up to the moment I landed," replied the doctor. "I have broken *rapport* now because it is unnecessary."

They found Bordeen and Joto with several of the captains, examining the Olban airship, while members of the crew eyed them rather suspiciously from the deck above.

Introductions over, Harry Thorne invited them aboard. "Ride with me to Reabon," he said. "We have every comfort and convenience and plenty of room for all."

He led them up the aluminum steps and along the deck to the foremost glass cab. Bordeen called down to his captains to resume the march, and the ship rose majestically as they entered the snug, glass-enclosed room, with its luxurious cushioned seats and thickly carpeted floor.

When all were seated a slave brought them steaming liquor in golden cups. "And now that we all assembled," said Harry Thorne, "I should like to ask Grandon why we are going to Reabon and what we are supposed to do when we get there."

Grandon drained his cup and handed it back to a waiting servant.

"The Princess of Reabon has been compelled to sign away her fortune and her hand. Speaking for myself and my Fighting Traveks, we go as her escort to do her bidding, no matter what may arise. To me it is almost inconceivable that she will meekly submit to Destho; yet if that be her intention, neither I nor any of my men will raise a hand to stay her. If, on the other hand, she should, at the last moment, decide to free herself from Destho and regain her lost throne, we will be ready to fight for her to the last man."

"You have spoken for the warriors of Granterra and their commander as well," said Joto.

"And for the Imperial Air Patrol of Olba, if I and my men may be included," declared Harry Thorne.

"It seems," said the doctor smiling, "that the princess does not lack allies. As to whether she will call on any of you or not — who can say? A woman's mind . . ."

"Is past understanding for any man, on this planet or another," interrupted Vorn Vangal. "However, I do not believe she will call for assistance. That proclamation, once signed, is binding alike on herself and her subjects. She might nullify any ordinary proclamation by issuing another, but in this case such a proceeding is quite impossible. She has named another to rule over her and her subjects; he, and he alone, can now nullify the proclamation."

"In that case," said Joto, "there might be ways of persuading him."

"A worthy suggestion, Joto," proceeded Bordeen, "but hardly practical; we cannot cope with the mighty armies of Reabon for any long period of time. The army of Reabon is the largest and best equipped in all Zarovia, and her soldiers know not the meaning of fear. Should Vernia decide on a revolt against the new emperor we could undoubtedly get her out of the country alive — a revolt against the emperor would make her a traitor and an outcast. Under the constitution of Reabon, which has prevailed for ages, she could never hope to regain her throne and scepter. When we reach Reabon she must choose between freedom as an outcast from her country forever, or the half of her throne which the proclamation still allows her, and virtual slavery to her emperor."

"Vorn Vangal speaks the truth," said Bordeen slowly, "for well do I know the unchanging laws of Reabon and the regard in which they are held by every subject of the empire."

"In that case," said Dr. Morgan, "it seems that further discussion of the problem is futile. It rests with her majesty to choose, and with us to act only when she has made her decision."

"Quite right," agreed Thorne. "And now that the subject has

been dispensed with for the present, Doctor, suppose you tell us a few things I have been itching to find out ever since I received your telepathic summons to meet you here, through Vorn Vangal. You have had quite an advantage over Grandon and me, you know, being cognizant of our every moment since we left the Earth, while we know nothing of what you have done since we last saw you."

"As we are nearing Reabon I will only touch on a few points that may be of interest to you," said the doctor. "Both of you will be surprised to know that the Zarovian men who exchanged bodies with you have committed suicide, destroying your Earth bodies by leaping from a precipice. I did not communicate the reason to you, but it will become apparent from what I am about to relate.

"The Olban prince whom you represent, Thorne, and Prince Thaddor knew something of the exploits of both of you on this planet. The former became despondent while the latter grew insanely jealous of Grandon. They formed a suicide pact, and stole away together one moonlight night to carry it out. Their — or more exactly, *your* — mangled bodies were found the next morning at the foot of the cliff."

Morgan sighed. "In a few days I start my return journey to Earth. I will be happy to have either or both of you join me if you care to do so, though I fancy that Harry Thorne will not care to leave, and that Grandon's decision to go or stay will depend on what takes place in Reabon today. When I am ready to start I will let you know, and you will have until then to make up your minds."

"Mine is made up right now," said Thorne. "You couldn't drive me away from this planet with a pack of man-eating hahoes. There's a little girl back in Olba . . ."

"Tell us about her, and some of your adventures," said Grandon.

They were interrupted by a call from the lookout. Thorne stepped out for a moment — then returned. "My story will have to wait," he said, "for we have arrived in Reabon."

CHAPTER XIX

Grandon and his companions, peering over the rail of the airship, saw that they had indeed arrived at the capital. Immediately below them was the procession consisting of a string of vehicles and carts now led by the one carrying Vernia, and accompanied by the two small armies of Uxpo and Granterra, the latter with its strange, fierce sabit cavalry, the like of which had never been seen before in Reabon.

From their point of vantage they could see that the city walls were lined with spectators, as were both sides of the main thoroughfare leading to the palace. The gates were slowly lifted, their powerful motors hummed sonorously, as the vehicle of the princess approached.

When it passed the gates a mighty cheer went up from the assemblage and the colors of Vernia flashed out suddenly, waved by a hundred thousand hands. Then, as if in obedience to a single word of command, every man, woman and child in the vast multitude bowed low, with right hand extended palm downward.

The crowd that lined the broad avenue, soldiers and civilians alike, remained on bended knee until the vehicle of the princess passed them, then rose and waved her colors once more.

As the triumphal procession approached the palace gates the throngs rose, and the inmates, from the highest to the most lowly, did homage.

A golden palanquin carried by four kings greeted the vehicle as it arrived at the palace steps. Two slaves parted its scarlet curtains and Vernia stepped within, motioning Rotha to follow. The curtains fell back in place and the multitude rose and cheered vociferously as the palanquin with its imperial burden was carried through the palace doors.

The air fleet, which had been hovering above the palace grounds, slowly descended. As Grandon and his companions reached the foot of the aluminum stairs, one at a time, they were met by a palace guard who inquired their names and titles and assigned a slave to each man to conduct him to his quarters.

Grandon had been amazed by the size and beauty of the imperial palace as viewed from without, but even that marvelous sight did not prepare him for the glory and magnificence he beheld within. As he followed his guide, a beardless youth clad in purple of nobility and evidently serving as a sort of page while learning the customs of the court, Grandon gazed in wonder and admiration at the rich decorations and furnishing. Even the corridors through which they passed were paved with blocks of agate and jasper, polished like glass and faultlessly fitted together, while the sides and ceiling were of alabaster inlaid with designs in pure gold and set with mural panels done in oil and rimmed with platinum, each one a priceless work of art.

At length they came before a door of highly polished wood of reddish hue, studded with bolts of gold. On each side of this door stood a soldier attired in the brilliant raiment of the imperial guard and armed with tork, scarbo, and broad-bladed spear.

Both bowed low with right hand extended palm downward, as Grandon came before them. Then one rose and flung the door wide and the other drew back a heavy scarlet curtain behind it.

Grandon entered, followed by the page. The curtain fell behind them and the door was softly closed. The room they were in had evidently belonged to a huntsman and warrior of no mean accomplishments. Its paneled walls were hung with weapons and trophies of the chase and battlefield, and skins of marmelots and ramphs, magnificent specimens, were flung on the floor. A ramph, carved from the red wood and supporting a round top of polished crystal, formed a huge table in the center of the room.

Two chairs, one on each side of the table, were cut from the same red wood to represent kneeling giants holding the curved scarlet cushions that formed the seats and backs.

Immediately adjoining this room, and separated only by an arched doorway with scarlet hangings, was another, even more luxuriously furnished and elaborately decorated. It was lighted, as was the first, by two enormous windows reaching from floor to ceiling. Between them was a massive sleeping shelf over which hung a scarlet canopy with a golden fringe at its edge. Two chairs, a table smaller than the first, and three huge chests or wardrobes completed its furnishings.

Grandon's guide led them directly through this room to a magnificent bath which formed the third and last unit of the suite.

The ablutions over, the page provided him with a suit of scarlet apparel from one of the huge wardrobes, and a slave brought a tray containing a pot of fresh-brewed kova and an endless variety of choice viands.

Grandon invited the page to participate in the feast, but he declined with thanks, saying it was not seemly that he should eat at the same table with royalty.

"You have been employed in the palace for some time, have you not?"

"For nearly two years, your majesty."

"Ah. Then perhaps you can tell me who formerly occupied this suite."

The page looked at him in amazement.

"Can it be possible that you do not know whose rooms these were?" he exclaimed. "This is the private suite of Emperor Margo, the mightiest of all emperors of Reabon and sire of our beloved Princess Vernia."

Grandon was dumbfounded. "Where is the new emperor named in the proclamation of the princess?" he asked. "Where is Prince Destho?"

"The Imperial Proclamation will not be read until high noon today. Prince Destho is in the palace in his own suite."

There was a rap at the door and the page hastened to answer it. In a moment he admitted Bonal, Vernia's pompous prime minister. That portly individual bowed low with right hand extended palm downward, then stood stiffly erect and delivered his message.

"It is the command of her Imperial Majesty, Vernia, Princess of Reabon, that Grandon of Terra, King of Uxpo, attend her at once in the audience chamber."

Grandon followed the officer through a maze of corridors and passageways, then through an arched doorway between two guards who saluted stiffly as he passed, and found himself in the audience chamber.

The door through which he had entered was at the right of the throne — a door which royalty alone was privileged to use. He was escorted to a position among the scarlet-clad members of the Reabonian royalty, from which he had an excellent view of the entire hall.

He could see Bordeen, Vorn Vangal and Dr. Morgan standing with the purple-clad nobles. As the doctor wore a purple uniform it was apparent that he had been created a noble of Reabon.

Below them in lines of the blue-clad commoners her could make out Oro and Rotha, and the uniforms of many Fighting Traveks as well as the glistening armor of the Granterrites. Across form him, clad in the scarlet of royalty, he saw Harry Thorne, Joto, and somewhat apart from them, the triumphantly grinning Prince Destho.

The buzz of conversation ceased abruptly as the scarlet curtains the surrounded the throne slowly parted and slid majestically back to the wall in shimmering folds, announcing the coming of the princess.

Then the massive doors at the end of the hall swung open and the imperial procession entered, headed by the four kings who bore the palanquin, and followed by Orthad, Supreme Commander of Reabon, who carried on a scarlet cushion the huge jeweled scarbo that was the scepter of Reabonian authority.

After him came a hundred members of the Imperial Guard with gorgeous uniforms and shining weapons, who ranged themselves in two straight lines reaching from the foot of the throne to the end of the hall.

Then, for the first time, Grandon saw how a ruler of Reabon mounted to the throne.

Orthad presented the imperial scarbo which she took from the cushion and rested across the arms of the throne. Her gaze swept the assemblage and her eyes rested for a moment on Grandon. But it became plainly apparent in a moment that Vernia had no intention of asking assistance, for she summoned Bonal, her prime minister, and ordered him to read the proclamation.

As Bonal faced the crowd and unrolled the document with an exaggerated flourish, Grandon looked across at Prince Destho, and noting the look of triumph in his dark eyes with difficulty restrained himself from leaping across that narrow space and throttling the man.

The prime minister stepped to the edge of the dais and read:

"A Proclamation by Her Imperial Majesty, Vernia, Princess of Reabon.

"On the twenty-fourth day of the eighth Endir in the four thousand and tenth year of Thorth, I, Vernia of Reabon, hereby proclaim and declare to all my subjects throughout the length and breadth of the empire that I have taken for my husband, and raised to the office of emperor, to rule over me and my people, the brave and illustrious Grandon of Terra.

"It is my command that copies of this proclamation be made and distributed to all parts of the empire without delay, and that the fifth day of the ninth Endir be set aside as a day for feasting and suitable celebration in honor of this momentous event.

"Vernia, Princess of Reabon."

Grandon could scarcely believe the testimony of his own ears; a glance at Prince Destho showed that he was no less amazed.

A ringing cheer broke from the throats of the vast multitude: "Long life to Grandon of Terra, Emperor of Reabon!"

Grandon stood still until a young prince plucked at his elbow and whispered: "Step before the throne."

He followed this sound advice and waited, stiffly erect while Vernia descended and gave the imperial scarbo into his keeping.

"Mount to the throne," she bade him in a whisper, "and place the scarbo across the arms as you saw me . . ." Suddenly she paused with a scream of terror. "Look behind you — quickly!"

He whirled in time to see Destho, his face contorted with rage and his scarbo descending in a shimmering arc. There was no time to parry the blow; Grandon leaped aside, then caught the blade with the imperial scarbo, twirled it and sent it clattering to the floor.

His weapon gone, Destho turned and sprinted for a side door. Soldiers ran to intercept him, but before he reached them a man attired in a bloody, tattered uniform leaped out from the ranks of the commoners and caught him by the beard. "Thus should all traitors die!"

As the words rang clear above the tumult, a knife flashed in the hand of the soldier, then thrust into the breast of Destho.

Grandon arrived to see the plotter lying on the floor with bloody froth issuing from his mouth and trickling down on his wiry beard. His assailant had fallen across his prostrate body, and Grandon recognized Zueppa. The wound inflicted on Zueppa by the man he had just slain had been reopened by the exertion. In a moment both were dead.

Four soldiers removed the bodies and order was restored with surprising celerity. Again Grandon moved to the foot of the throne where Vernia awaited him, wide-eyed and trembling. He took her hands in his for a moment, then she resolutely bade him proceed.

Upon his return the four kings had prostrated themselves on the steps leading to the throne in accordance with the customs of their ancestors. Grandon turned to Vernia. "I am emperor now, am I not?"

"Assuredly, my lord."

"And my word is law?"

"So long as it does not conflict with the written constitution of Reabon."

"Is this matter of mounting the throne on the backs of one's vassal kings written into the constitution?"

"No. It is a custom that has been observed for generations and signifies the complete submission of the heads of the various kingdoms."

"Then it shall be abolished. I expect loyalty from my subjects, but not abject servility."

Then, to the surprise of the four kings, he bade them rise and stand, each man on the step he occupied, two to the right and two to the left. Thus attended, Grandon mounted to the throne while the spectators looked on in amazement.

When he had taken his seat with quiet dignity and rested the scarbo across the arms of the throne, Vernia mounted and bowed before him with right hand extended palm downward — an example which was followed by the entire assemblage. It was indeed a day of surprise for the good people of Reabon, for no sooner had she knelt before him than he, in violation of an age-old custom which decreed that the empress should sit at the feet of her lord, swung the scarbo to one side and lifted her up beside him on the throne.

"You shouldn't have done this," she gasped. "My place is . . ."

"Custom be hanged!" he responded, and there, in full view of that vast multitude, he kissed his bride full upon the lips.

The crowd responded with a resounding cheer. "A long and happy reign to our emperor and his empress!"

Then the shimmering scarlet curtains crept around the throne, and Grandon forgot all else when two soft arms stole around his neck and Vernia's fluffy head nestled on his shoulder.

"I don't understand about the proclamation yet," he said, at length. "How and when did you manage to change it?"

"It was changed before I affixed my signature," she said, "else I should sooner have died than sign it. While Destho's attention was momentarily drawn to you I crossed out his name and substituted yours. I then allowed the scroll to roll half downward, as if by accident, and when he turned he saw that I was signing and, happily, never bothered to unroll it again!"

At a loss for suitable words to express his admiration and adoration, Grandon sought refuge in banality. "You wonderful little woman," he said.

At midnight, two weeks later, Grandon and Vernia stood on the roof of their palace watching the movement of a metal cylinder that was slowly screwing itself into place in a huge sphere of asbestos and steel.

Bordeen had left that day for Uxpo with the Fighting Traveks. Oro, Rotha, and Tholto had accompanied Joto and his Granterrites back to their people in the Valley of the Sabits, and Harry Thorne and Vorn Vangal had flown from Olba, as the former Martian was anxious to be with a certain beautiful princess who awaited him.

They had bidden Dr. Morgan good-by after helping him into his ponderous diving suit, had watched him clamber aboard, draw up the ladder and close the cylindrical door, and now waited to see his remarkable interplanetary vehicle begin its journey back to Twentieth Century Earth.

At length the cylinder clicked into place, and Grandon signaled two attendants, who flashed a powerful searchlight on the sphere.

Slowly it rose, rocking gently at first like a toy balloon on a flexible wand. Then, with a suddenness that was appalling, it shot swiftly skyward. The searchlight swung upward, groped about for a moment, making a flashing spot of light on the fleecy clouds, and then found its objective. In that incredibly short time the sphere had traveled so far as to have the diminutive appearance of an orange. A moment later it was but a tiny pinpoint of white. Then it disappeared.

Grandon ordered the light shut off and turned to go, when Vernia laid her hand on his arm.

"Look," she said. "Your world is our moon."

He looked, and for a brief moment was vouchsafed the glorious spectacle of the Earth and her satellite, through a break in the clouds — the most brilliant and beautiful sight in the nighttime of Zarovia.

Then he turned to the infinitely more lovely vision beside him, and together they descended the stairs.

THE END

www.ingramcontent.com/pod-product-compliance
Lightning Source LLC
Chambersburg PA
CBHW020143180626
46810CB00004B/1713